# LeeAnne James

# Murder at Gatewood

ARCHWAY
PUBLISHING

This is a work of fiction. All of the characters, names, incidents, organizations, and dialogue in this novel are either the products of the author's imagination or are used fictitiously.

Archway Publishing books may be ordered through booksellers or by contacting:

Archway Publishing
1663 Liberty Drive
Bloomington, IN 47403
www.archwaypublishing.com
1 (888) 242-5904

Because of the dynamic nature of the Internet, any web addresses or links contained in this book may have changed since publication and may no longer be valid. The views expressed in this work are solely those of the author and do not necessarily reflect the views of the publisher, and the publisher hereby disclaims any responsibility for them.

Any people depicted in stock imagery provided by Getty Images are models, and such images are being used for illustrative purposes only. Certain stock imagery © Getty Images.

ISBN: 978-1-4808-6523-5 (sc)
ISBN: 978-1-4808-6524-2 (hc)
ISBN: 978-1-4808-6522-8 (e)

Library of Congress Control Number: 2018910439

Print information available on the last page.

Archway Publishing rev. date: 09/11/2018

To my grandmother, Nana, who always said I should write a book

# Acknowledgments

I would like to thank my sister-in-law, Kelly, for being the first one to read the manuscript. You gave me the confidence to keep at it until it was published.

To my family, friends, and coworkers, thank you for the words of encouragement and support as I tried my hand at writing a novel. My emails may never be the same again.

And to Linda, who joined me on this adventure with both feet jumping in, I will forever be grateful for your creativity, but especially your friendship.

# Prologue

The pain came first. Then the lapse into semiconsciousness. He felt himself sag at the knees and then drop to the floor. He heard the thud of the brass bookend on the carpet next to his head. All was silent, except for his heavy breathing. In the distance, as if he were already in some other far place, he heard the soft padding of footsteps and the click of the door as it closed.

He was alone. No one would find him for several hours. His staff knew he liked to work in the predawn hours. His staff knew never to disturb him. Blackness swept over him like a swift incoming tide. He sank deeper into the darkness ... deeper ... deeper.

# Chapter 1

## 1880

It was a beautiful, unseasonably warm day in April, and Amelia Payne was enjoying the sunshine as she and her sister, Leah, strolled through the gardens of Hartwell Manor, their family's estate. Amelia always loved the spring because it was such a refreshing time. The air smelled crisp and fresh, the birds flitted from tree to tree and sang their beautiful songs, and leaves from the nearby trees fluttered softly in the gentle breeze.

Amelia looked at the beauty all around and couldn't help smiling. It was hard to tell what part of the gardens she liked best. Was it the hedgerows cut into perfect angles and rows so that when she walked to the center of the maze she'd find the iron benches that surrounded her favorite marble fountain? Or was it the flower gardens that always had an endless spray of colors throughout each season?

She paused to look at their large manor house with chimneys poking up from each of the four corners of the roof. Amelia loved the redbrick house with its wide steps that led invitingly to the heavy front doors and the ivy that climbed up the sides, seeming to defy gravity. Amelia was glad she didn't have to pick her favorite part of the estate. It would have been an impossible task since she loved it all.

The estate was located only a few miles outside of London, and she knew their family had the best of both worlds. They enjoyed the country setting and preferred to use Hartwell Manor as the main family home, but they could take a short carriage ride into London to enjoy the sights and activities that the city had to offer. The family would often stay at their townhome in London, especially during the social season. But Leah and her husband, Emmons, stayed at the townhome year-round because, unlike Amelia, they preferred the hustle and bustle of the city to the quiet serenity of the country manor.

Amelia was filled with excitement, barely able to keep from skipping down the paths that wound among the foxglove, crocuses, and rosebushes. Now that she was eighteen years of age, her debut would take place the following night. She had been planning this for months, making sure everything—her dress, her hair, and the ball—would be absolutely perfect. Amelia would be officially introduced to society, especially all the eligible bachelors. She was hoping for a match this season. But not just any match. She had her eyes set on Sir Herbert Woodford, Duke of Brazelton.

Woodford was five years older than she was, making him even more alluring with his chocolate-brown eyes flecked with gold and his dark, wavy hair that seemed to shine like the sun. For her own part, Amelia knew she was a catch for the men. She had noticed how men of all ages soaked in her hourglass figure, beautiful auburn hair, piercing dark eyes, and smile that lit up the darkest of nights in the pale cool light of a full moon. When she looked in the mirror, she admired her angular nose, high cheekbones, and sculpted chin. She knew she was inwardly prideful about her good looks, and she didn't care one whit about false modesty.

Amelia broke into a smile as she remembered when she had met the duke two years before at Leah's wedding. Leah married Stanley Emmons, Earl of Clayborne, and Woodford had stood up with the couple at their ceremony. Woodford and Emmons had met at university and become instant friends, making their rounds of the local drinking establishments and creating good-natured mischief whenever they could.

Since the wedding, Amelia enjoyed seeing Woodford as often as she could. Most of the time, it was when Leah hosted a dinner party. Now that she would be having her coming-out, Amelia would be able to enjoy the theater, balls, and parties of the season, and she was looking forward to seeing Woodford more often at the various functions.

"Where has your mind gone to?" questioned Leah. "I've been talking to you for the last few minutes, but your mind is somewhere other than on our conversation. We need to finalize the details of your debut tomorrow night."

Amelia's cheeks flushed. "Why, I've been thinking of the duke, of course." She reached for a newly opened blossom and held it to her nose, enjoying its fragrance. "He tends to show up after the party has started, but I'm hoping tomorrow will be an exception. I would very much like it if he got there early enough that he could join me for my first dance." She smiled at her sister and laughed just a little. "I think we should get back. We need time to dress for dinner."

Leah giggled. "You're right. This will be your last supper."

"Don't say that! This will be the end of the beginning and the beginning of the new."

The sisters turned and walked toward the house. The rest of the late afternoon and evening passed in a distracted blur. And before she knew it, Amelia was waking up in the dim light of early dawn. She scrambled out of bed and yanked on the bellpull.

It took only a moment for her lady's maid, Rose, to appear at the door. "Yes, milady? Was there something you have a need for?" She had to stifle a yawn as she looked sleepily at Amelia.

Amelia crossed the floor as light as a dancer and grabbed Rose's hands before the maid even realized what was happening.

"Oh my, ma'am!" Rose laughed as she and Amelia twirled around the room, the hems of their dresses barely touching the woolen rug under their feet.

"Tonight is the night, Rose! After my coming-out, I will finally be able to go to the fancy luncheons and tea parties with the other ladies. And to the grand balls. And, best of all, I'll be able to dance with a certain gentleman named Herbert Woodford, Duke of Brazelton." Amelia let go of Rose's hands. "I'm sorry, Rose. I didn't mean to make you feel uncomfortable."

Rose laughed. "You know me better than that, Miss Payne. After all, it's an exciting time."

Amelia thought back on how much Rose had been through before she found her place at the Payne estate. Ten years Amelia's senior, Rose was twenty-eight, with a small build, light complexion, mousy brown hair, and dark eyes that always seemed to have a bit of sadness reflected in them. Her mother had died during Rose's birth, and her father, an aging bookseller, couldn't give Rose the home she deserved and needed. Rose had no choice but to leave home and find work as a housemaid.

Luckily Rose was offered a position at the Payne estate, where she scrubbed the floors and dusted the household's many rooms. But in no time at all, she had forged a genuine friendship with Amelia and became the young lady's maid. It certainly helped that Rose was skilled at sewing and had a talent for weaving her lady's hair into the latest styles.

Rose helped Amelia slip into a fresh day dress and pin up her hair. As she sat in front of the vanity mirror watching Rose pin the curls in place, Amelia's mind wandered to the conversation she'd had with her mother, Sophia, the previous night. They had talked about how so much was dependent on a debutante's introduction into society these days in the hopes of attracting a suitable husband.

Most marriages were based not on love but on a political alliance of sorts. Families looked for their children to marry within the same social standing, preferably someone with a title but never someone beneath their own title. A man needed to find a wife who was strong and sturdy enough to give him an heir to carry on the family name, and if he were lucky, the woman came with a large dowry.

The woman generally wanted to find a man who could provide for the family and was wealthy enough that he could ensure that she maintained the lifestyle that she was already accustomed to. Finding the right match could be an exciting yet very difficult and strategic time.

Amelia knew that her parents were an exception and were lucky with the love they'd found in their own union. They had met when they were very young and remained friends as they grew up. By the time they had reached the age to marry, it was a fait accompli that they would marry. It was wonderful to know that Sophia and Douglas, the Duke of Chatham, were very much in love—then as now.

This was a day like no other, and Amelia was anxious to get it started. The first order of business after getting dressed was a bite to eat for breakfast, although she wasn't very hungry.

*Perhaps I could just have a cup of tea*, she thought. Amelia fairly flew downstairs to the breakfast room. She knew if her mother had seen her, she would be chastised for running on the stairs because that was something proper ladies didn't do. But the day was exciting, and it was difficult for Amelia to adhere to the rules of society, especially in her own house with no one but family at home.

She found her mother and sister already seated at the table with plates of eggs, toast, and ham slices in front of them. Amelia poured a cup of hot tea and took her seat at the table, right across from Leah.

"You'd better have something to eat," warned her mother. "It's going to be a very long and busy day, and you'll need to keep up your energy."

"I couldn't eat a thing. I'm too nervous. Besides, if I'm not careful, I'll never fit into my gown tonight!"

As she spoke, her brother-in-law walked into the breakfast room and let out a laugh as he headed toward the sideboard where the food was spread out. "Take care, sister. You'll never find a husband if he knows he can't afford to feed you!"

Amelia tried to frown at him, but she knew he was only teasing her. She finally gave in to a laugh. "If I can't find a husband," Amelia joked, "I'll just have to live at the townhome in London with you and Leah."

Emmons groaned and turned toward the food to make his selection, but not before Amelia saw him wink at Leah.

The rest of the day passed quickly as the preparations were made for the debut. Flowers and candles filled the large ballroom, leaving the air heavy with a wonderful fragrance that was a mix of spring flowers and beeswax. One portion of the room in the far corner was left clear for the orchestra while tables and chairs lined the outer edges of the room, leaving plenty of space in the middle for dancing. The marble floor had been polished to a high sheen and would reflect the candlelight as if it were as bright as day inside the room. Amelia's father spared no expense when it came to his daughters, and he was determined to make this an affair to remember. The town would be talking about this debut for ages.

Later that afternoon, Amelia started to get herself ready. Rose prepared a hot bath scented with lavender in the dressing room, and

Amelia felt some of the tension of the day subside as she soaked in the tub. Next, she waited while Rose pinned up her long auburn hair in an intricate design that left lengths of curls to fall gently, almost touching her shoulders. Rose added a bit of baby's breath and ribbon that seemed to enhance the color of the curls in her lady's hair.

Finally, Rose brought out Amelia's satin gown, the color of perfectly ripe lemons, with a floral design hand-embroidered in white stitching on the bodice and hem, with pearls and sequins sewn into the pattern. The yellow of the dress brought out the highlights in Amelia's hair and the blush on her cheeks. There was no doubt that Amelia was a beautiful woman, and tonight she would be the most attractive of all.

At last, the time had come. Amelia smiled as her father took her by the arm to the receiving line. Guests were already arriving.

"Don't be nervous, Amelia," her father said. "This is just a party, an event to celebrate you."

"I'm not nervous, Papa. I am so very happy. Thank you, Papa, for making this night so special." Amelia stood on tiptoe to kiss her father on the cheek.

Every time the heavy wooden doors opened, Amelia watched with nervous anticipation to see whether Woodford would be on the other side, but she was disappointed each time.

Before she knew it, it was time for her to make her official debut. With one last look at the doors, she turned away and headed toward the ballroom, her eyes downcast. She was very disappointed. She'd had her heart set on Woodford being there right from the beginning of the ball.

As she stood outside the doorway to the ballroom, Amelia and Rose looked one last time to make sure everything was in place, ensuring that none of Amelia's hairpins had fallen out and she was as perfect as she could be.

With a deep breath, Amelia walked into the ballroom on her father's arm, smiling at the many friends who had gathered for her special evening while trying to hide her disappointment that Woodford wasn't there. The room absolutely sparkled from all the wonderful clothes and jewelry that shone under the chandeliers.

Suddenly toward the back of the room, she saw Woodford and gasped. Their eyes locked, and everyone else disappeared for Amelia. If her father hadn't been holding her arm, she would have stopped walking, but he put his hand on her back and managed to gently propel her forward.

*How did Woodford get in without my seeing him?* Amelia broke out into a wide smile. *He's here! Woodford is here for the first dance of my debut!*

He made his way toward her, and it seemed like she couldn't even breathe. Just as he reached her, the orchestra started playing music for the first dance, a waltz. The duke reached out and gently took her hand. Before she knew it, she was in his arms, dancing the first waltz of her debut with the man she had dreamed about. Amelia had never felt happier in her entire life as he held her in his arms and they gazed into each other's eyes.

# Chapter 2

The bright sunshine woke Woodford up. He groaned, feeling his head throb from the hangover. Even the single bird singing outside on the rooftop hurt his head. He lurched out of bed, rested his elbows on his knees, and groaned again.

He thought a little hair of the dog might silence the pounding between his temples. On the other hand, he figured a hot cup of coffee and some toasted bread with jam might be better. Woodford stood up, waited for the room to stop spinning, and made his way to the door.

"Flanders, where in bloody hell are you?" He closed his eyes as the sound of his own voice reverberated in his head.

"I am here, Your Grace. Would you like your bath readied?"

Flanders, the duke's personal butler, had been with his family for many years. A tall man, he had salt-and-pepper hair and was still muscular at forty-five years of age. He was very good at his job, so much so that the other staff members looked to him for guidance and direction. The duke knew that Flanders was the reason the household ran as smoothly as it did.

"Yes, but I need sustenance. While the water is heating, bring me some coffee and toasted bread with elderberry jam, please." The duke groaned and put his hands to his forehead, as if that would still the pounding in his head.

Woodford stepped back into his chambers, padded across the floor, and lay back down on his bed. The fog in his brain started to lift, and he smiled as he thought about last night. It was hard to believe he had danced with Amelia, holding her in his arms as they danced to the music that he didn't even seem to hear. His mind was completely on her, how beautiful she was and how she seemed to be as light as air as they swept across the floor. No dancing partner had ever matched his steps the way she did. They fit together perfectly.

In the last two years, he had watched with increasing interest as Amelia grew from a young lady into the stunning woman she'd become. Every time he saw her, he was more and more attracted to her, with her long, wavy hair, her lips the color of pale roses, and her gorgeous brown eyes that made him catch his breath every time she looked at him.

She wasn't a mindless ninny the way some of the debutantes were. He could talk to her and have an intelligent conversation that wasn't just about the weather. She listened to him as he talked about the farms on the estate, and he listened to her as she talked about the latest book she was reading or the news in the daily papers. They shared stories with each other about everything under the sun, and there was rarely a lull in their conversations.

Now that she had her debut and was properly introduced to society as an available young lady, he could officially start courting her. In fact, he would start by dropping by this afternoon to see her and make his intentions known.

After a refreshing soak in the tub and a rejuvenating breakfast, Woodford headed for the study and the ledgers. This was the part of the job that he didn't particularly like, but the estate had been left to his care after his father had passed away three years before. He would much prefer to ride his favorite stallion, Pegasus, across the wide lands of the estate, watching the crops grow and the sheep graze in the fields. There was something gratifying about seeing the hired hands working with the land and the animals and seeing it all grow and come alive under their care.

If he could, Woodford would be out there with them, but his position as the only child meant that, upon his father's death, he had inherited and now ran the estate. Unfortunately for him, the societal rules would not allow him to work the fields alongside the hired help. Because of that, Woodford always felt like something was missing in his life, that something was just out of his reach, like a carrot dangled in front of a stubborn mule. He longed to spend his days outdoors, but it wasn't meant to be. Men of his station in life didn't dirty their hands. They hired other people to do that for them.

After working for a few hours on the ledgers, Woodford got up from the desk and stretched. The sun was high in the sky as it was peeking through the damask draperies, telling him that it must be getting toward noon. He decided he needed to hurry if he were to catch Amelia at home. He hadn't told her yet of his plans to court her, so he wanted to see her today, hoping they could have a chance to talk privately. He was fairly confident that she felt the same for him as he felt for her, but he wanted there to be no misunderstanding. He wanted to make sure there would be no other suitors vying for Amelia's attention and possibly her heart.

Woodford had a stable hand saddle Pegasus for the ride to the Payne estate. Normally it was only a brief ride since the estates neighbored each other, but today he was anxious to get there and set the horse to a good pace. Thoughts of Amelia kept him company on the ride and pushed him faster and faster.

Once at Hartwell Manor, he brought his mount to a stop, ran up the wide stone steps, and barely had a chance to grab the heavy iron door knocker before Perkins, the butler, opened the door for him.

"Good afternoon, Perkins. I'd like to see Lady Amelia, please."

"One moment, Your Grace. I'll see if she's available."

Perkins had been with the Payne family for many years, and Woodford thought that Perkins, with a touch of gray hair at his temples, was probably approaching fifty years old. He also knew that Perkins was as good at his job as Flanders was at his. *What would the families ever do without them?* the duke wondered.

Perkins showed Woodford into the parlor, but he was too anxious to sit or stand still. He began pacing back and forth with his hands clasped tightly behind him. To settle his nerves, he stood at a window, looking out over the garden as the birds flittered from one bush to the next. *How beautiful the gardens are here.* He was proud of the gardens at his own estate, but these were even more beautiful.

He turned around when he heard a gentle rustling noise at the doorway. When he saw Amelia standing there, his eyes widened. She was wearing a beautiful satin dress of hunter green that showed off her perfect figure. From her neck hung a small golden locket that shimmered with each breath she took.

"Your Grace, how lovely to see you." A broad smile broke out on her face as she gave him a gentle curtsy and delicately tipped her head.

"Lady Amelia, you're looking as stunning as ever. Could I interest you in a walk through the gardens so I might talk to you privately?"

Amelia's eyes lit up. "If you give me just a moment, I'll grab my wrap."

Woodford waited anxiously for Amelia to return. He paced back and forth in front of the expansive windows in the parlor.

"We're ready," Amelia said, coming up behind him.

He felt the gentle touch of her hand on his right elbow. He turned and saw that Rose was with her, but of course she would be. It wouldn't be proper for Amelia to be totally alone with him without a chaperone.

"Shall we?" He offered his arm.

"Yes, we shall."

He could feel the warmth of her hand on his arm as he led her outdoors. *It feels so right having her next to me.* He was aware of Rose, but he was also pleased that she stayed a respectful distance behind them, allowing their conversation to remain private.

He exchanged small talk with Amelia as they made their way into the gardens and then headed into the maze. As they approached a marble bench next to a tall hedgerow, Woodford motioned for Amelia to sit down.

He sat next to her, took her gloved hand in his own, and gazed longingly into her eyes. "Lady Amelia, I have waited for what has seemed like an eternity for your debut. Before anyone else has a chance to step in, I would like to make my intentions known. I would very much like to court you, if you would allow me to."

Amelia nodded her head hard enough that the curls hanging over her shoulders bounced. "I would like that very much, Your Grace."

Woodford gently lifted her gloved hand and kissed her knuckles softly, never taking his eyes off hers. Amelia touched the spot on her hand that he had just kissed and held his gaze with her own.

Amelia sat quietly with Woodford on a bench overlooking the back gardens. The mild summer evening was like most others of late. It seemed that the days since her debut had all blurred together. She spent her time going to parties and balls, playing cards, or snuggling up near the fireplace with a good book when the cold rains swept in off the Atlantic, making it necessary to light a fire even in mid-July.

She sighed. *Life somehow doesn't satisfy.* She couldn't put her finger on the reason for her growing discontentment, but it was there.

"Woodford," she said.

He looked over at her. "What, my dear?"

"Lady Margaret is having a little party. It's nothing fancy. But I'd like for us to go."

He scowled. "I'm growing bored of parties, fancy or not."

"But, Woodford, I haven't seen my friend Lady Margaret in over a month. You see, her parents and mine are the best of friends, which is how I came to know her. But since we've been going to functions with your friends all summer, I haven't seen most of mine except occasionally. Couldn't we visit with Lady Margaret tonight?"

"My dear, I've already made plans for us tonight. We're going to see my friend Lord Thomas and play whist with him and his fiancée, Lady Harriet."

"Are you sure we can't go see Lady Margaret and her parents? I've truly missed them."

"No, Amelia, and that's final. There will be no further discussion on the matter."

She looked at him, puzzled by the look of satisfaction he seemed to have on his face, but she turned away so he didn't see her disappointment and confusion.

Amelia excused herself, saying, "I have to get dressed for dinner."

After they ate, they went to Lord Thomas's mansion, where Woodford proceeded to ignore her. She fought back the sadness that suddenly washed over her as she watched him slowly get drunk.

Not long after that night, they were attending a ball when

Amelia realized that he did seem to be enjoying his drinks quite a bit, which quite disturbed her. She hadn't noticed before how much of a drinker he was, but she had to admit that he seemed to hide it well. She only noticed now because he would reach for a glass as the servants passed by, and she came to realize that he was reaching quite often.

One afternoon, Amelia confided her concerns in Leah when they had a quiet moment together. "Sister," Amelia stammered, "I may be overly concerned, and it may not be a problem, but it seems to me that Woodford drinks quite a bit more than I realized. Have you noticed that?"

"Now that you mention it, I have heard gossip among the ton that he's known to be a drinker and enjoys his spirits. But I don't believe you need to worry. After all, Emmons is one of his dearest friends, and they were known to drink quite heavily when they were out together, but now that we're married, Emmons has cut down considerably. He may have one or two bourbons at a social function, but that's it. He rarely has more than that. I think you'll find that, once Woodford settles down a bit, he'll do the same."

"I hope you're right, Leah." Amelia sighed. "I've never felt that drink adds anything likeable to a person's character."

Woodford had been spending most of his afternoons at any of the local drinking establishments or at his friend Emmons's home in London, but no matter where he spent his time, it always involved an excess of drink.

All the social functions were wearing on him as well. Frankly, he'd become bored with the routine. Amelia was a real beauty, and he liked having her on his arm. But the woman could be tiresome, especially when she mentioned his drinking habits. On the other hand, he could do a lot worse when it came to finding a wife, and he was actually quite fond of her.

Now on a cool afternoon in September, he found himself being escorted into her father's library. He knew Amelia had gone shopping with her sister. That suited him. In fact, he'd arrived at the Payne estate early on purpose, knowing he would still have plenty of time before he met her for dinner.

"Good afternoon, Lord Payne," he said after Perkins announced him.

"Good afternoon, Woodford. What brings you around on this fine day?" Amelia's father stood up and motioned with his hand for Woodford to take one of the chairs across from his desk.

Although a large man, Douglas Payne was well known for his gentle, fun-loving nature and his smile. The members of the ton liked him well enough, and he was well respected for his keen business sense. It was common knowledge that he was willing to share his business advice to anyone who asked, and more times than not, that guidance had often led to lucrative investments.

"Well, Your Grace, as you know, I've been keeping company with Lady Amelia for quite some time now. I believe we would be a good match together, and I've come to ask your permission for your daughter's hand in marriage."

Payne sat at his desk, twirling a pen he'd been using between his fingers. "Do you love my daughter?"

"Yes, sir, I do. I have since I first met her more than two years ago. And I will see that she wants for nothing and that her every need is met. I will do my best to make her happy."

Payne looked down at the papers on his desk. He hesitated long enough that the duke started to wonder if Payne would say no. *Is Lord Payne upset with me?*

Finally Payne spoke. "I knew your father since before you were born, my lad. He was a fine gentleman. I think he would be happy with the match. As am I."

"Thank you, sir! Thank you!" Woodford jumped out of the chair and reached for Payne's hand over the desk, pumping it vigorously. "I will speak to her tonight. You have made me a very happy man indeed."

Woodford almost ran for the door, but he slowed long enough to turn around and look back at his future father-in-law. The older gentleman was smiling warmly.

When Woodford arrived in his carriage later that evening, he jumped down before it had come to a complete stop. He took the steps two at a time and lifted the knocker, banging on the door, once, twice, three times.

Just as Woodford was impatiently reaching for the knocker again, Perkins opened the door. "If you'll wait in the parlor, Your Grace, I'll fetch my lady for you."

It was only a moment before Amelia appeared. Woodford felt a warmth in his heart as Amelia entered the parlor. She was wearing a sapphire blue evening gown with an elegant choker around her neck and matching bobs that dangled from her ears. The large blue stones were the same hue as her dress. Rose had twisted Amelia's hair into an intricate braid that wound around the back of her head, almost like a halo.

Woodford thought she was breathtaking. He took her gently by the hand and led her to the settee. He bent down on one knee in front of her as her eyes opened wide.

"Amelia," he began, using her Christian name, "you are the most beautiful woman I know. I have loved you since I first saw you at your sister's wedding more than two years ago. I'd like to spend the rest of my life with you, if you'll have me."

Amelia's hand covered her mouth, and tears fell down her cheeks as she struggled to speak. "Yes, Woodford, yes. Definitely yes!"

He gently lifted her left hand and placed an exquisite gold ring on her finger. A large, deep-red ruby was in the center, surrounded by five small diamonds and five small rubies, each small stone alternating one with the other.

She stared at the ring on her finger and tipped her hand just enough that the stones reflected the sparkle of the gaslights in the room. "It's beautiful, Woodford! Just beautiful!"

Both stood up, and she flung her arms around his neck as he grabbed her around her waist. Their lips met, and at that moment, Woodford was the happiest man in England. He'd dreamed of marrying Amelia since he first met her more than two years earlier. Now his dream would come true.

They had the banns read at church for three consecutive Sundays, and the invitations were sent out. The wedding was to take place at Hartwell Manor on Christmas Eve, a time that was especially festive and beautiful to Amelia. They would be expecting about two hundred guests, so the staff had been busy for weeks, preparing for the wedding as well as the holiday festivities. Two large fir trees graced the foyer with red and gold ribbons tied to the ends of the branches. Garland was wrapped along the banister of the grand staircase, and poinsettias graced the tables scattered throughout the home. Candles were glowing from every window of the manor while chandeliers shone from above. Snow had fallen lightly the day before, leaving a glittering white cover over the trees, grass, shrubs, and hedgerows. Even nature had helped to transform the estate into a beautiful winter wonderland.

Leah and Emmons stood as witnesses to the marriage, as Amelia and Woodford had with them. Amelia was dressed in a peach chiffon gown that shimmered in the candlelight, and a small diamond tiara sat perched on her head to hold the long train of lace that flowed behind her. Woodford wore a dark brown tuxedo with tails and a crisp ivory shirt with matching waistcoat and cufflinks of gold. His silk cravat was the same shade of peach as Amelia's gown.

For the wedding feast that followed the ceremony, the cooks had prepared lamb, roasted goose, and suckling pig. There would be potatoes, turnips, cranberries and stuffing, mince pies, sweetmeats, and Christmas pudding flaming with brandy. It was a wonderful feast, fit for royalty.

The newly married couple dined with their guests and danced until the early morning hours. It was a magical time that couldn't have been any more perfect. Eventually the last guest left, and Woodford tucked Amelia's hand into his elbow to escort her upstairs to their chambers. The December night was too cold to travel to his home, so they took the largest suite in the manor, normally reserved for distinguished guests. Tomorrow they would move to the duke's home as husband and wife.

As Woodford moved to take Amelia in his arms, she could smell the bourbon on his breath and noticed the slight stumble in his steps. She hadn't been watching, but she didn't realize he'd had that much to drink. But all thoughts of drinking left her mind as soon as he kissed her and led her to the bed.

# Chapter 3

## January 1881

The wedding was only just a few days past, but Amelia found herself in a world she had only dreamed about. As the new year came in with a fresh round of parties, she was now the Duchess of Brazelton, the lady of Gatewood Castle. Although it was known as a castle for as long as anyone could remember, it really wasn't a castle but rather a large manor home with brick walls and plenty of windows, all surrounded by lush, beautiful gardens.

Thankfully Amelia's father had allowed Rose to come with her, and having her there helped Amelia feel more comfortable in the new surroundings as she adapted to becoming the lady of the house. She hadn't realized how many decisions she was responsible for, but that was probably because her mother was so good at running the Payne household while Amelia was growing up that she made it look easy.

Her first order of business was to meet the servants who worked in the castle. She already knew Flanders, but there were still quite a few more to become acquainted with. She immediately took a liking to Cook, a rather round lady, probably about sixty years of age, with a wonderful disposition and a warm smile. Amelia learned very quickly that Cook was excellent at whatever she prepared in the kitchen and had no doubt that she would have to watch what she ate, or she'd be letting out the waistline of her dresses very soon.

Woodford had given Amelia carte blanche to redecorate the many rooms of the castle as she liked, but there was very little that she wanted to change, at least right away. His parents had cared for the castle very well, and she could see a subtle feminine touch—obviously his mother's—throughout the home. Although some of the rooms appeared dark because of the wood floors, paneled walls, and mahogany furniture, the hallways, dining room, and ballroom were bright and cheerful with marble floors and light-colored walls. For the most part, Amelia would leave things as they were for now. She decided that she would add her own touch by having flowers brought in from the conservatory and displaying them throughout the home.

She decided that she would like to redecorate the parlor, generally the room where the family would greet their guests, so she wanted it to be more inviting and brighter. It only had two windows and appeared to be very dark with heavy brocade drapes and dark-colored muslin on the furniture.

Amelia arranged to have the walls papered in a luscious cream color with a pattern of thin burgundy stripes while the furniture was covered in deep red velvet. The combination seemed to give the room a warmth that it hadn't had before. Once it was all done, Amelia and Woodford were both pleased with the results.

Amelia also chose to redecorate her suite of rooms. They had been furnished with heavy furniture and dark wallpaper, but she preferred a softer look. She arranged to have the walls covered in a soft pink paper with thin gold stripes, giving the room a delicate feminine appearance. The paintings that hung on the walls in thick gold frames were mostly of flowers and hilly countryside. The same shades of soft pink and gold found on the walls could also be found in the damask draperies, bedclothes, and carpets, although they also had other splashes of color that seemed to enhance the vibrant colors found in the paintings. It all blended together perfectly, and she enjoyed spending time in the brightness of her rooms.

Although spring was quickly approaching, the weather was too chilly to be outside in the mornings, so Amelia preferred to spend her free time reading from the large supply of books in the duke's library or practicing her music on the pianoforte in the grand ballroom. She enjoyed singing and playing the pianoforte, and oftentimes Woodford would join her. Although he preferred to just sit and listen to her, he would occasionally join her in singing a song, which pleased her immensely.

Woodford would spend his mornings in the study, poring over the leather-bound ledgers of the estate and studying the financial reports of the farms. He would need to make sure that enough hay, wheat, and corn was planted for the farms to be sustainable. He hoped that quite a few of the sheep and pigs would become pregnant, which meant there would be money coming back to the estate once the offspring were sold.

Then for the afternoon, they would get together to enjoy a quiet tea and perhaps a stolen moment of intimacy. But Amelia started to notice that Woodford still managed to polish off a good many drinks by evening. She had hoped that this was only a passing fancy for him. After all, the old castle was a bit drafty, the weather was chilly, and a drink helped to keep the soul warm.

*Perhaps he won't drink as much by springtime,* she thought. *He'll be busier than ever with the farms and hopefully won't have the desire or time to drink. Yes, I'm sure of it. Things will be different by spring.*

They had been planning a honeymoon to France but decided to wait until after the holidays when the weather promised to be better for traveling.

Finally after the first week in February, the weather was warm, and the roads were clear. The trunks and valises were loaded onto the coach, and they set off for four weeks in Paris.

Amelia felt truly buoyant as she and Woodford passed the time in Paris, embraced in the lap of luxury. They stayed in the grandest hotel and ate at the finest restaurants. They went to shops, museums, and shows. While she didn't often indulge herself in the past, she couldn't resist buying a selection of the most elegant clothes from the finest shops in the city.

Woodford, a doting husband who spared no expense for her happiness, took great pleasure in allowing her to order as many clothes and accessories as she wanted. Very quickly, boxes of the many beautiful things that she had purchased began to fill their rooms.

Then things changed one night when they were at the opera. A man approached them in the lobby. Amelia could see that he'd been drinking.

"Good evening," the man slurred as he stood in front of them, weaving a bit. He seemed focused on Amelia as his eyes lingered on her décolletage. "This promises to be a memorable show tonight."

"Do I know you, sir?" Woodford stepped protectively closer to Amelia's side, pulling himself up to his full height.

The man ignored Woodford and let his eyes linger on Amelia as she tried to politely take a step away from him.

"If you'll excuse us, sir, my husband and I are going to find our seats now."

The man stepped in front of her, blocking the way while leering at her and licking his lips. "Why don't I find us a nice booth where we can watch the show together?"

Woodford grabbed Amelia roughly by her elbow, sidestepping the man and growling at him, "If you know what's good for you, you'll keep your distance from my wife."

After the encounter with the drunken man, the evening at the opera was ruined. They sat in the palatial box seat high above the common crowd, but Amelia found her thoughts were elsewhere. She couldn't concentrate on the opera. She had never seen Woodford's gruff side. *Yes, the man had been annoying but was obviously inebriated*, she thought.

When they got back to their suite in the hotel, Woodford was still angry. Amelia stepped into the dressing room to put on her nightdress. He grabbed the bottle of bourbon, poured himself two fingers, and gulped it down. He poured himself another, this time filling the glass, and stood in front of a window that overlooked the city.

Amelia approached him quietly and gently placed her hand on his shoulder. "Why are you so angry, my love?"

Woodford whipped around, spilling the amber liquid from his glass, and glared at her. "I didn't care for the way that man was looking at you. You are my wife, and I'll not have you on display."

"Oh, Woodford. The man was obviously in his cups, and I'm sure he had no idea what he was saying. He probably won't even remember it in the morning." Amelia flicked her hand, as if to show that it was nothing to be concerned about.

"You are mine and mine alone!" he bellowed.

Before Amelia could even respond, he grabbed her and forcibly pushed her toward the bed. She felt his lips pushing hard on hers and heard the tear of her cotton nightdress. It was over in a matter of minutes.

She couldn't even look at him as she lay there, the tears flowing from her eyes. Her lips were swollen from his kisses. She could feel the bruising down below where before she had felt such warmth and pleasure from their being together. She never ever thought he was capable of such brutality.

Amelia rolled over and closed her eyes, praying that sleep would come and she'd wake up in the morning and chalk this up to just a bad dream, a terrible nightmare that she could cast away with other bad dreams and hopefully forget about.

But morning came, and Amelia knew it wasn't a dream. Woodford had spent the night awake in a chair, staring out the window at the moon and stars over Paris, still in the clothes he had worn to the opera. She had silently lain awake all night as well, huddled under the silk sheets and wearing a torn nightdress.

Just as the sun started to rise, she felt him sit on the side of the bed, but she pretended to be asleep.

He gently put his hand on her shoulder. "Amelia, I know you're awake. I beg your forgiveness. I don't know what came over me. When that man was looking at you in that way, I felt an emotion I've never experienced before. I just wanted to protect you."

Amelia turned to look at him. "I know it is a husband's right to take what is his, but please know that I am terribly hurt, both physically and emotionally, by what you've done. My love for you is strong. There is no need for you to be so forceful with me ever again."

They clung to each other. Woodford held her tightly while tears spilled from her eyes onto his shoulder.

They returned home from Paris with boxes and trunks piled high on the carriage. Rose helped Amelia unpack the baggage, carefully hanging the new gowns in the armoire so they wouldn't be crushed. As Amelia opened yet another box, Rose's reactions delighted her. She knew that her steadfast and reliable servant thought that each gown was prettier than the last.

"These gowns are stunning, my lady! I can't believe how exquisite they are! You will be the envy of the ton!" Rose held each gown up to herself and twirled in front of the full-length mirror like a ballet dancer on a music box.

Amelia couldn't stand the suspense any longer. She pulled a beautifully decorated box from the heap and gave it to Rose. Inside was a golden cameo brooch, its filigree edges decorated with seedling pearls.

Rose could hardly breathe as she looked at the gift, the most beautiful thing she'd ever owned. "Oh, my lady. It's beautiful!" She carefully pinned her new brooch to her gown and admired herself in the mirror. "I will treasure it always!"

From that day forward, Rose was rarely seen without the cameo brooch proudly adorning her dress.

The next day, Sophia and Leah came for a visit to welcome Amelia home. They sat in the parlor enjoying tea with shortbread and lavender cookies that Cook had freshly made that morning. Amelia was learning very quickly that Cook and the rest of the kitchen staff at Gatewood were extraordinary in their skills. If she weren't careful, she would have to have her new Parisian gowns let out.

Her mother and sister listened as Amelia told them all about Paris, the shows, the museums, the people, and the food.

"Leah, you would love the shops. They're just filled with the latest styles of dresses and hats, and everything is so beautiful. I tried hard not to act like a giddy schoolgirl and stare at the ladies walking by, but everywhere I looked, I was in awe. And Mother, I know you would enjoy watching the most popular plays and shows. It seemed as if there was something new to see at the theatres every night. But I think Father would have enjoyed the meals the most. The selections of delicious food were endless. I don't believe I've ever eaten so much in my life!"

They listened intently as Amelia told them everything, except for what had happened that one horrible night. She was trying so hard to forget about it, so there was no point in tarnishing her memories of that magical time of their honeymoon. And if no one else knew, then surely in time, Amelia would forget as if it never happened.

⌢

Finally the winter months gave way to spring, and with the new season came news. Amelia and Woodford were enjoying a quiet dinner together one evening. Their conversation was light as they talked of his plans for the farms on the estate.

"There will be another addition to the estate as well." Amelia looked at him, waiting for his reaction.

"Are you with child?" His eyes opened wide at the idea.

"Yes, my love. I am." She could feel the tears of happiness welling in her eyes.

He jumped up from the table, almost knocking over his chair and startling the footmen waiting by the door. He enveloped her in a warm, strong hug that lifted her out of her seat. Both laughed with joy at the news.

"Are you pleased?" she asked him.

"I couldn't be any happier! When will the child be born?"

"Toward the end of October. I believe the blessed event happened while we were in Paris."

Woodford couldn't be happier. *My wife is expecting a child, the most precious gift of all.*

After dinner, they went into the library, Amelia picking up an embroidered sampler she'd been working on while Woodford smoked a cigar and enjoyed his brandy. He was so excited that he kept pacing back and forth, not knowing quite what to do.

*I am going to be a father, and if it is a boy, I will have an heir. But even if it is a girl, I will love the child the same,* he pondered.

They talked about whether it would be a boy or a girl, what would be possible names, and which schools the child should go to, all the things that new parents were excited to talk about.

Amelia had already started to plan things out. "We'll have to prepare the nursery, but I don't want it on the third floor. I prefer it on the second floor, right next to our rooms. We could put it across the hall from our bedroom, and if we should need one, the nanny can stay in the room next to that."

It was customary for the children of society and nursery staff to be in rooms away from the parents' rooms while the children were young, but Amelia would have none of that. She would make sure that both Woodford and she were very much involved in their child's life. The idea of pawning off her child for another woman to raise was appalling to her, and she wouldn't even consider it. That was the way she was brought up, and that was the way she would raise her children.

The following day, Amelia and Woodford rode in the phaeton to the Payne family home for dinner. Leah and Emmons had been at the country manor visiting for a few days, so it was a perfect time to share the news of the pregnancy with them as well as her parents while everyone was still together.

They had gathered around the dining room table for a simple meal of beef pie, roasted potatoes, and biscuits. The conversation was light with lots of laughs and good-natured teasing. Just as the dessert of strawberry pie was being served, Amelia found the lull in the conversation a perfect time to make her announcement.

With a smile, Amelia lifted her wineglass. And as everyone looked her way, she said, "I'd like to make an announcement. Woodford and I are to be parents. I am with child."

Her mother clasped her hands to her breast with tears in her eyes, her father jumped out of his chair to shake Woodford's hand, Emmons patted Woodford on the shoulder, and Leah squealed with delight as she hugged her sister. The idea of a new babe in the family was wonderful news. Everyone was talking at once, laughing, crying, and hugging each other.

After dinner, the ladies went into the parlor, full of excitement and chatter about the baby. The men, meanwhile, went into the library for a cigar and an after-dinner brandy. They talked of their farms, politics, and, of course, the baby.

Before they knew it, it was later than Woodford and Amelia realized, but it was hard to break up the gathering. They were having such a good time after sharing their news with the family.

The summer months passed quickly. There had been many social events to attend during the summer season, but before she knew it, the time came for Amelia's confinement. Then one cool September afternoon, she and Rose were passing the time by rearranging the flowers in the dining room. Amelia had always taken great pleasure in bringing a bit of the outdoors to the indoors whenever she could, and fresh flowers was one of the best ways.

Amelia felt a sharp pain and gasped. She wrapped her hands around her belly as Rose looked at her in surprise.

"Is it time, my lady?"

"I don't know for sure, but I believe so. The pains are rather uncomfortable."

"How long have you been feeling these pains?"

"Since this morning, shortly after breakfast, but I didn't want to say anything until I knew for sure that the baby was coming."

Rose put her arm around Amelia and tried as quickly and carefully as she could to get Amelia to her bedroom.

On the way, she stopped Flanders. "Please fetch the doctor.

The baby is on its way. You must find the duke as well. Let him know that it's time for the babe."

Flanders first set out to find the doctor, whose home was located on the edge of the estate. Luckily Dr. Kerr was in, so he grabbed his medical bag, jumped in his carriage, and made for Gatewood. Flanders then headed into London to try to locate the duke.

Woodford lifted another pint in the pub, a small tavern known as the Hammer and Sickle. He had tried to stop drinking. He even went for long walks along the secluded path that snaked through the woodlands at the edge of his property. But nothing seemed to work.

Woodford took a long swallow, emptying his glass. Suddenly he saw Flanders appear at the door of the pub.

Flanders hurried over. "Sir, it's your wife. The babe is coming."

Woodford felt a surge of joy, an elation he'd seldom experienced before. "Are you sure?"

"Yes, sir! As sure as the sun rises and sets."

Woodford was so excited that he shouted, "The next round is on me! C'mon, men! Join me in a quick drink to welcome the birth of my firstborn!"

Each man surrounded Woodford as all came up to pat him on the back and join him for a toast to his child.

Flanders leaned in close. "Sir, you're needed right now. The babe is coming. It's not likely to want to wait on you or even the heavens."

As soon as Woodford made it home, he ran up the steps two at a time and knocked on the door to his wife's bedroom. Rose opened the door but tried to keep Woodford from coming in.

"This is no place for a man when his wife is giving birth. But if you'll wait downstairs, Your Grace, we'll send word as soon as the child appears."

"Bloody hell! Let me see my wife, and then I'll leave her be."

He pushed past Rose, knocking her to the side, and went to the bed where Amelia lay. Sweat covered her, and her hair stuck to her face, but she had never looked more beautiful to him. He wiped her brow with a cool cloth, gave her a gentle kiss on her forehead, and went downstairs to wait.

Flanders had sent a footman to let her family know about the impending birth, and it wasn't too long before Emmons and Leah arrived. Leah pulled her gown into her hands and took to the stairs as quickly as she could to be with her sister, while Emmons joined Woodford in the library.

For the first time in months, Woodford had something else to think about other than his own troubles. Today he would drink, but for an entirely different reason. This time he was drinking to celebrate, not to forget what could never be.

Finally, after what seemed like ages, the child, a healthy and hefty son, was born. Woodford, after hearing the child's first cry, ran upstairs. Rose and Leah met him with a smile, and as he walked in the room, he saw his beautiful wife holding the baby.

"You have a son, my love. A fine, handsome son." Sweat still shone on her brow and dampened her hair, but he had never seen her look lovelier.

Overcome with emotion, Woodford seemed rooted to the spot, but when Amelia gently lifted his son toward him, Woodford found his legs and walked toward the bed.

"He's beautiful. You're both so beautiful." He held his son as a tear fell gently down his cheek.

# Chapter 4

## 1882

Herbert Douglas was growing strong and healthy. He had been a fast crawler but was now learning to walk and getting into everything, as babies often did. Amelia found that, as much as she hadn't liked the idea, she would need help with Herbert. She was still trying to run the household and keep the social commitments required of her as a duchess, as well as keeping a good eye on Herbert, but there just wasn't enough time in the day for all of it. She made the decision to ask around for a good governess, and one of her friends recommended a niece of hers who happened to be looking for employment.

Mrs. Aubrey Parker was middle-aged and married to a nice man named David, but they had not been blessed in having children of their own. Aubrey had worked for many years as a governess and came with very good references. David, who also came with excellent recommendations, was hired on as the estate manager. And as it happened, there was a vacant cottage on the estate that Aubrey and David could move into. Aubrey would help Amelia during the day but would be able to return to their cottage in the evenings to fix dinner and spend time with her husband. But if necessary, Aubrey was close enough that she could lend a helping hand at any hour of the day or night if Amelia should need it.

It wasn't long before Amelia found out she was pregnant again. When she told Woodford, he was ecstatic. He loved Amelia dearly and would now have two children to love and spoil as well.

Life with Amelia was certainly different than anything he could have imagined. *Maybe life isn't so bad after all*, he thought. He still had the urge to be a farmer in the truest sense of the word, but it would never happen the way he wanted—no—needed it to be. On the other hand, he found out that having a household filled with family was wonderful. He had grown up without siblings and with a mother and father who were very distant from him. They believed in the adage that children should be seen and not heard. They rarely hugged each other, had very little conversation between them, and simply existed in the day-to-day functions each had to perform. His father ran the estate; his mother was always attending one charitable event or another. And as soon as he was old enough, Woodford was shipped off to boarding school. He'd come home on holidays but as he got older only when he had to.

Then one day, when Amelia was about three months pregnant, a footman from Hartwell Manor came racing on horseback to tell them that Amelia's mother had taken ill with an apoplectic spell. Amelia and Woodford quickly climbed into the family carriage and took off, leaving Mrs. Parker to take care of Herbert.

Perkins met them at the door with a worried look on his face that Amelia had never seen before. "Your mother is upstairs in her chambers. The doctor is with her now."

Amelia ran up the stairs as fast as her slippers would carry her, while Woodford went into the library to check on his father-in-law. Payne was sitting at his desk, staring at his hands, which he had wrapped tightly around a glass tumbler. Woodford went to the liquor cabinet and poured himself a drink. Amelia's father still hadn't looked up, so Woodford quietly sat in one of the leather wingback chairs that faced the desk. They sat together in silence. The only sound was the slight sipping noise as Woodford nursed his bourbon, while Payne only stared at his.

The elder man was lost in thought. He couldn't bring himself to acknowledge his son-in-law as he sat down. He used to be very fond of the lad, but over time, he found he liked him increasingly less.

*He had us fooled*, thought Payne. *I hadn't realized what a drunkard he is. I just hope he treats my daughter well. She deserves a loving and sober husband.*

As he sat there, the elder man let his mind take him back in time to when he first met and fell in love with Sophia. She was as beautiful thirty-five years ago as she was today. She had always been the love of his life, and he couldn't imagine what his life would be like without her in it. The idea that she might die left him heartbroken in a way he'd never felt before.

After a half hour or so, Dr. Kerr came downstairs. "I'm sorry, Your Grace. There's nothing more I can do. It's only a matter of time."

Payne looked up, his face ashen, and nodded to the doctor. Very slowly, he stood up and made his way upstairs to his dying wife.

As they walked in the room, Amelia's father saw his family gathered around his wife as she lay on the bed. Amelia and Leah were sitting in chairs next to the bed with each holding one of Sophia's hands. Woodford walked in right behind Payne and went to stand next to Amelia. Emmons was already there, standing next to Leah. They stayed that way for a long while, not talking, just quietly listening to Sophia as her breathing slowed. Finally, as they all waited for her next breath, they realized there wouldn't be another. Sophia Payne, Duchess of Chatham, beloved wife, mother, and mother-in-law, had passed away.

The next few days were difficult yet busy as Sophia was laid out for the viewing in the parlor and an endless procession of well-wishers came to Hartwell Manor. She was interred in the family cemetery with a headstone that paid homage to the loving and respected woman that she was. It was, without a doubt, the most difficult time in their lives.

While they went through the motions on the days following Sophia's death, Leah and Emmons clung to each other for comfort, while Amelia tried to be a comfort to her father. But the truth was that they leaned on each other, and without realizing it, that left Woodford to be cast to the outside. He tried to be there for Amelia, but he found it difficult to do. He had never been especially close to his own parents, but in the years since he'd known the Payne family, he had grown quite close to Douglas and Sophia. He found that he was hurting in a way he wasn't familiar with and didn't quite know how to handle the emotions stirring inside of him.

He decided that if he couldn't figure out what to do with his own emotions, he was certainly no use to anyone else and their emotions. The solution, once again, was to drink and try to escape.

A week after the funeral, Amelia was sitting in the library at Gatewood, staring at the pages of a book without even reading it. The words could have been written backward, and it wouldn't have made any difference to her. Suddenly she felt a terrible pain in her abdomen, so strong that she doubled over. The book clattered to the floor as Amelia gasped with pain. Rose was just walking in with a tea tray when she saw her lady doubled over in the chair. She nearly dropped the tray but managed to set it on a table just inside the door.

Rose screamed, "Flanders!" She rushed to Amelia's side and

knelt on the floor, trying to look into Amelia's eyes and understand what was happening. "My lady, what is it? Is it the babe?"

Amelia could only look up and nod her head, still clutching her belly with shaking hands. Flanders came rushing in, took one look at Amelia, and ran to her side. He gently picked her up and started for her chambers upstairs.

"Call for Dr. Kerr," Flanders firmly told a nearby footman as he walked by with a pale-faced, shaking Amelia in his arms. As he entered the hall, he ordered another footman, "Alert the duke. He is in his study."

Once Woodford heard of his wife's condition, he raced upstairs to be with Amelia. He found her lying in bed in the fetal position, clutching her stomach. He rushed to her side and knelt on the floor next to her.

He tenderly wiped her damp brow with his hand, and as her tears fell, he gently wiped each one off her cheeks. "My love, what's wrong? Have you eaten something that doesn't agree with you? Shall I have Cook make you some tea? Perhaps a soothing tonic?"

Amelia could feel the warm, sticky wetness between her legs and knew without looking that it had to be blood. She was losing the baby but couldn't bring herself to tell him. She closed her eyes to the pain and look of unanswered questions in her husband's eyes.

When the doctor arrived, Woodford waited in Amelia's sitting room, while Rose stayed in the bedroom with Amelia during the examination.

Dr. Kerr confirmed Amelia's fear. "I'm so sorry, Your Grace. You've lost the baby. I believe the stress of your mother's passing was just too much on the child. However, I'm confident that you will be able to have more children in the future. I realize that this news will do little to make you feel better now, but in time, I think you'll see things a bit differently."

Dr. Kerr gave Amelia a warm look of compassion, tipped his hat to both Amelia and Rose, and then left.

Losing the child had been devastating for Amelia, and she fell into a deep depression. In the days and weeks that followed, she refused to venture out of her chambers, not even bothering to get dressed in anything other than her bed clothes. She either stood at the window for hours on end or remained in bed, deep under the covers. She shunned the company of Rose and Woodford, preferring to eat her meals alone. If she ate anything, it was merely a few sips of broth or a nibble of bread, barely enough to sustain a bird. It seemed no one could say or do anything that appeared to have any effect on Amelia's melancholy until one day her young son came to see her.

As he walked into her sitting room, he found his mother staring out a window that overlooked a beautiful garden of different-colored roses. He walked up to stand next to her, not uttering a sound. He simply put his small hand in hers and stood there silently, looking out the window with her. After several minutes, she became aware of her son's hand in hers, and she looked down at him, frowning, as if she couldn't understand who he was. His big brown eyes looked back at her, and he smiled. Suddenly it was as if a dark veil had been lifted from her mind.

She blinked back the tears that welled up in her eyes while looking down at her son. "Herbert! Oh, Herbert! I am so sorry. I've missed you. I shouldn't lament so over a child that's been lost when I have a beautiful son right here. A son to love, to hold, and to cherish."

Amelia knelt and took Herbert in her arms. She hugged him and kissed his rosy cheeks and soft brown hair that smelled like a little boy. How she had missed him, and yet she hadn't even realized that she had until now.

∽

Where her son was concerned, Amelia was happy. But his father was a different matter altogether. Early one evening, Amelia stared glumly out the windows at the back garden, lost in thought. She once loved the beautiful greenery, the birds, and the look of the sun when a cloud shadow passed. Now though, the garden's beauty made her feel even emptier.

She got up, crossed the room, and poured herself a glass of water. She returned to the window, and her anger began to build. She'd seen how distant her husband had become even before she lost her child. But the distance was worse … much worse.

No matter what she said or did, Woodford pulled away and refused to say why. He went through the motions of being a husband and keeping up appearances by going with her to the parties and balls, but his heart was not in it. He seemed angry and despondent, and he was drinking quite heavily. That certainly did not help. She decided she would confront him once and for all.

While they were sitting in the library after dinner, she gathered up enough nerve to ask him what caused him to be so melancholy and angry. He was looking out the window with a drink in his hand when she approached him from behind.

"What's wrong, my love? What causes you to be so upset? Would you talk to me, please?"

He didn't answer her but continued staring out the window into the darkness.

Amelia moved to his side and gently put her hand on his arm. "Please?" she asked softly.

"It's not anything you would understand." He would not look at her.

But she could tell that his brow was creased into a frown. "How do you know I wouldn't understand? Perhaps I'll surprise you.

Please talk to me and see if I understand. I'll wager I understand more than you think I might." She hoped he would see the love and concern she had for him.

Woodford whipped his head around to look at Amelia, but she stepped back, surprised at the anger in his eyes. She had never seen him like that, and it scared her.

"I told you that you wouldn't understand. You don't know what it's like to be a man in this world. You don't know how god-awful life is when you have no choices. When a man must do what's expected of him, what he was born to do, not what he wants to do. Do you know what that's like? No, you don't, so don't tell me that you would understand." His voice had gotten increasingly louder until he was shouting at Amelia.

Suddenly he threw the glass in his hand at the fireplace. Amelia watched in horror as it shattered into a hundred pieces of shining crystal. Her husband brushed past her, knocking her out of his way as he left the room. She stood there wide-eyed and with her mouth open, looking at the door.

She could not believe what she had just witnessed. *What was happening to my husband?*

Amelia gave birth to a second child, a beautiful girl named Charlotte. Amelia made the decision, as difficult as it was for her, to focus more on the children than on her husband. After all, she could not do much if he refused her help. And yet the children needed their mother, and she needed them.

Although Amelia took a loving interest in the children and spent as much time as she could with them, their father wasn't much more than a passing stranger in their lives. If he were home, he spent his time in the solitude of the study and usually had his meals served to him in there.

But more often than not, he would leave Gatewood by late morning and not return until late at night, well after the children were in bed. Woodford and Amelia were by now staying in separate bedrooms, only occasionally sleeping in the same bed.

One autumn afternoon, Amelia was nursing three-month-old Charlotte while Rose folded and put away the linens that had been freshly laundered. Herbert Douglas was in the next room with Mrs. Parker, just finishing up his school lessons for the day. Herbert was a very energetic child, always moving to and fro, but he was also very serious about his studies. Lessons with Mrs. Parker were about the only time that he sat still. He particularly enjoyed learning his numbers and reading, but he seemed to have a knack for languages as well, and he was learning to speak a bit of French.

After Amelia put Charlotte to bed for a nap, she headed downstairs, walking Mrs. Parker, who was headed home, to the door. Just as they reached the bottom of the grand staircase, she was surprised to see her husband coming through the front entrance. It only took a moment for her to realize that he was very intoxicated. He couldn't stand straight, his clothes were disheveled, and she could already smell that he stank of sour ale.

"Good day, my lady," Mrs. Parker said and slipped past Woodford on her way out the door.

She kept her eyes on the floor, only glancing at Woodford and offering a small token curtsy as she brushed past him. Just then, his young son came bounding around the corner but tried to stop short when he saw his father at the door. Unfortunately his five-year-old legs were not quick enough. He tripped, went sprawling across the floor, and crashed into a small three-legged table.

The table tipped over and, with it, a large porcelain vase holding a bouquet of sunflowers. The vase hit the marble floor and smashed to pieces. Thankfully Herbert was not injured, but he struggled to control the tears that formed in his eyes. He lay on the floor and looked between his mother and father, biting his lower lip to stop it from quivering.

In an instant, his mother was beside him, lifting him up in her arms. "Oh, Herbert, are you okay?" she asked as she looked him over.

"I think so, Mama. I'm just clumsy is all. I'm so sorry about the flowers."

"We can always get another vase and pick more flowers, Herbert. You're all right, and that's all that matters."

Woodford watched the scene unfold and grew angrier by the second. "You must learn to be more careful, Herbert. Come with me."

Amelia held on to her son tightly, not letting him go. "What are you doing? Where are you taking him?"

"I'm going to teach him a lesson. He needs to learn that he can't go running through our home like he's some sort of street urchin."

Amelia kept her eyes on her husband and her arms around her son. "It was only an accident."

"Let go of him, wife! He's my son, and I need to teach him to be a man."

Before Amelia even realized what was happening, Woodford stepped in front of her and slapped her across the face. Stunned, she took a step backward, still managing to hold on to Herbert. But her young son wriggled out of her arms. He was not going to allow his father to hit his mother. He pounded his small fists as hard as he could on his father's stomach.

"Stop it! Don't hit my mother! Don't do that to her!" The boy kept pounding his fists on his father, but with not enough strength in his five-year-old body to do any damage.

The elder man grabbed his son by the wrist and dragged him

outside toward the stables. Amelia ran after him, but her husband pushed her away.

"Get away! He needs to learn what it is to be a man!"

"Woodford, let go of him! He's only a boy! He didn't mean any harm. He just tripped!"

Once again, Woodford pushed Amelia away, this time with enough force that she almost lost her balance. He reached for the door to the stables, pushed his son inside, and slid the wooden bar into place, locking the door behind them.

Amelia stood outside, banging on the door and pulling on the handle, but it wouldn't budge. She could hear the switch as it whistled through the air and the sickening snap as it connected with her son's body.

Amelia screamed, "Woodford, let me in!"

But if he heard her, he did not acknowledge. By then, some of the stable hands and groundskeepers had heard her screams and came running.

"Someone stop him! He's taken a switch to Herbert! He must be stopped!"

Finally, after what seemed like hours but was really only minutes, the door opened, and Woodford came out. He didn't look at Amelia or anyone else who had gathered at the stable door. He just walked toward the house with sweat covering his brow, and he was breathing heavily through his nose, like one of the bulls in the paddock.

Amelia rushed in to find her son lying in an empty stall, curled up in the hay. Lying next to him was the riding crop that his father had used to beat him. The back of his shirt was torn, and she could see the welts starting to develop on his back. She carefully lifted him up and held him as close as she dared. She turned to find Flanders and Rose standing there.

Flanders's arms were out to take her son. "I'll take him, my lady. We'll get him to his room." He gently took the boy with one arm under his shoulders and one arm under his knees, carefully carrying him back to their home.

Amelia kept pace with Flanders, who was rushing on his long legs to get Herbert inside. She could feel the flush on her cheeks from the anger she felt toward Woodford. *How dare he? How dare he take a switch to Herbert? It was a simple accident that did not warrant a punishment like that. Nothing deserves a punishment like that. Has Woodford lost his mind?*

When they got Herbert to his room, Rose had already brought in a bowl of cold water and fresh towels. Flanders sat him on the edge of the bed and helped him take off his shirt. As Herbert lay down on his stomach, Amelia held a cold, wet towel to his back to try to ease the pain. It was only then that Herbert buried his head in the pillow and softly cried.

Dr. Kerr arrived and set to work on dressing the wounds on Herbert's back. As the boy sat up on the edge of the bed, Dr. Kerr wrapped fresh linens around his torso. Thankfully, the welts were not bleeding so that would make it a bit easier when it came time to change the dressings. *Still,* Amelia thought, *there would be a lot of pain for such a young lad to have to experience.*

By the time Dr. Kerr left, Herbert's wounds were dressed, and he had a small dose of laudanum to help him sleep. Amelia, Flanders, and Rose stayed with the boy until he fell asleep and then went across the hall to Amelia's sitting room, leaving the door slightly ajar in case Herbert called out during the night. His father had left at a full gallop on horseback shortly after the incident, and Amelia knew he wouldn't be back for hours.

Flanders was at the sitting room door, ready to leave, when he turned to look sadly at Amelia and Rose. "Let me know if you or Master Herbert will be needing anything, my lady. I'll be in my room."

Amelia was grateful, and in his eyes, she could see the same hurt that she was sure was showing in her own eyes. "Thank you, Flanders. Thank you for everything."

Amelia watched as Flanders left, with his shoulders hunched over with the weight of what he witnessed this day.

It wasn't until three days later that Woodford returned to Gatewood. The slap he had given Amelia turned into an ugly purple and green bruise on her cheek, and his son was still in pain from the lashing he received. It would be a long time before they recovered from their wounds.

They stayed out of his way, and he stayed out of theirs. So they didn't see one another for a few more days. Then one day, Amelia was walking slowly in the garden, enjoying the sunshine and thinking about everything that had happened, when her husband approached her from behind. She sensed that he was there before she heard him, and when she turned around, he was standing only a few feet away. She could see him frown as he studied the dark bruising on her cheek that he was responsible for.

"How's Herbert?" he asked, barely speaking above a whisper.

"Slowly healing," she responded coldly.

"And you?" He tried to look into her eyes, but she wouldn't return his gaze.

Instead she found a small stone on the path that drew her attention. She played with it with the toe of her silk slipper. Then with a heavy heart, Amelia turned her back to him and started walking away. She did not want to talk to him, not after what he'd done. The drinking was one thing, but to strike her and take a whip to their son was an entirely different matter.

In two strides, he was directly behind her and put his hands on her shoulders. She stopped, and he gently turned her around to look at him. She did not resist, but she kept her eyes on the ground and tried to blink away the tears before he could see them.

"I'm sorry, Amelia. I don't know what happened. I had too much to drink, and when I saw Herbert knock over the table, I lost all control. I hope you can forgive me."

"I hope I can too, Woodford, but I'm not ready to yet." With that, she turned, gathered up her skirt, and ran back to the house.

Woodford stood rooted to the spot, watching her leave, until he heard the door closing firmly behind her. He knew at that point that more than one door had just been closed to him. He turned and almost ran to the stables, ordering a groomsman to quickly saddle up Pegasus. He mounted his steed and rode off as fast as he could get the horse to run. It wasn't until he heard Pegasus breathing heavily that he finally slowed.

He stopped at the edge of the creek, allowing Pegasus to cool down. Woodford sat on a large fallen tree trunk with his head in his hands. The guilt and shame were eating him alive. He'd beaten his son. He'd slapped his wife and left a horrible mark on her face. *How could I do such things to my family? What kind of monster have I become?*

Woodford looked back over the last few years. If he were being honest with himself, he could see that he had become more and more melancholy and withdrawn over that time. He knew the largest part of his despondency was because he felt trapped in a role that did not suit him. He was not meant to sit behind a desk all day, staring at numbers that did not make any sense to him. It seemed like he'd never been able to shake the desire to do something different with his life, to be able to work the land and not stare at the ledgers.

After all, he didn't have a good sense for business, and he knew it. He realized he even welcomed the final days of summer because that meant that his responsibilities to the farm would start to wind down until the next spring.

The fact of the matter was that Woodford did not like being a duke. He didn't care as much about the title, but it was the work that came with it that he didn't like. He just didn't have the mind for the facts and figures of running an estate. It all seemed to be a jumbled mess in his mind, and he could not care one iota about the number of bushels of wheat that were produced or the quantity of bales of wool that were sold. He preferred to work with his hands. He wanted to feel the fresh soil running through his fingers as the seeds were planted. He wanted to enjoy the feel of the soft wool as it was cut from the sheep. He would have liked to prune the hedgerows, cut down trees, and plant the flower beds. Working up a sweat and seeing the fruits of his labor would be exhilarating. That was what he really wanted to do, but it was something that would never happen, and it left him feeling empty.

The loss of his mother-in-law and then the miscarriage had devastated him. He never knew that kind of desolation until he suffered those losses, not even when his own parents had passed.

The only good thing he could say was that at least the estate was holding its own. It was not nearly as lucrative as it had once been when his father ran it, but his father had enjoyed his duties to the estate. To make up for some of the financial losses, Woodford had made some investments that his man of business suggested, but they had turned out badly. He should have gone to his father-in-law for advice, but he didn't want Payne to know that he wasn't doing as well as he claimed to be. That would be just one more embarrassment that he could not face.

And that was why he drank, to forget his unhappiness, that feeling that something in his life was missing. But it seemed like even that wasn't working anymore. It took more drinks to numb his mind, but he still was not able to forget his misery, regardless of how many drinks he'd had.

Woodford had been lost in thought along the side of the creek for a very long time. It wasn't until he heard Pegasus snorting that he realized the sun was starting to set. He gathered up the reins, stepped into the saddle, and turned his horse toward Gatewood Castle.

That night, he tossed and turned, unable to fall asleep. Finally, out of sheer exhaustion, sleep found him, but so did the nightmares. He dreamt that angry, hungry wolves were chasing him, nipping at his heels as he ran across the fields of the estate. The wolves all seemed to have coats made of pages from the ledgers rather than thick gray fur. It didn't matter how fast or which way he ran. The wolves threatened to overtake him.

He ran on and on, constantly looking over his shoulders to find the animals right behind him, with their coats of lined papers reflecting the silvery light of the full moon. Their growling and barking frightened him, making him run for his life to escape these wolves made of paper.

As the orange light of dawn shone into his window, he awoke, breathless and covered in sweat. The bedcovers lay at an odd angle across the foot of the bed where he had kicked them in his fitful sleep. He sat up, letting his feet find the solid floor of his bed-chamber. He reached for the pitcher on the nightstand and poured himself a glass of water. It had been a long time since he'd been that rattled from a nightmare.

Woodford fell into a deeper and deeper depression as time went on. His fits of rage got increasingly worse and were more frequent than ever before. Although he hadn't raised a hand to anyone since he'd beaten his son and struck Amelia, the entire household was still very wary of his temper. He would yell and scream like he was going mad. Amelia had no choice but to protect her children and herself by staying as far away as possible from the man she once loved with all her heart. Occasionally he would try to get into her room at night, only to find the door locked.

Finally he stopped trying altogether, and Amelia was secretly grateful that he hadn't tried to kick the door in. She had no doubt that, with his strength and the fury of his anger, the door wouldn't stop him if he really wanted to get past it.

One day while Amelia was working on her embroidery in the parlor, Woodford came in. She got up to leave, but he put out his hand as if to say, "Stop."

Amelia slowly sat back down but kept a cautious eye on him. After several moments, she asked, "What is it, Woodford?" She hoped her voice didn't sound as shaky as she felt.

"That's a very nice piece you're working on. You do such fine needlework, Amelia. Perhaps you can hang that in the parlor when you're finished. That way everyone can enjoy it."

Amelia's gaze dropped to the canvas in her lap. It was an intricate piece, modeled after the small creek that ran through the eastern edge of the estate. It was one of her favorite spots on all the estate, and she would often walk there in the early morning hours. When the rising sun reflected off the creek just right, the colors were stunning and brought a sense of peacefulness to Amelia.

"Thank you."

There was a stony silence for a few minutes as Woodford stood there, looking out the window while Amelia waited for him to say something. Finally he spoke. "I'm sorry, Amelia."

She didn't say anything, but there really wasn't anything she could have said anyway.

"I know I haven't been a good husband or father, and I want you to know that I'm truly very sorry. It was never my intention to act this way."

"Then why do you?" The words were out of her mouth before she could stop them.

With the bluntness of her question, Woodford turned toward her with a sad but distant look in his eyes. "Some things just can't be helped or made to be any different." And with that, he turned on his heel and left the parlor.

Amelia sat there, looking at the embroidery on her lap, wondering what he was referring to.

# Chapter 5

## 1889

Woodford was no longer living at Gatewood. Amelia knew he was staying at the townhome near Grosvenor Square in London, but that was no concern of hers. She rarely went to London anymore, but on the rare occasions when she did, she hadn't cared to stay at the duke's townhome anyway. Rather, if she went into the city, she preferred to stay at her own family's townhome with her sister and brother-in-law. If Woodford wasn't at Gatewood, life was better for Amelia, the children, and the staff, and that was all she could be concerned about. She didn't like to admit that fact, but it was an undeniable truth.

During the time that Woodford had been staying in London, Amelia found that she had no choice but to familiarize herself with the running of the estate. Her husband might have been gone, but the farms continued on and needed guidance. She learned about the finances by studying the ledgers. She learned from the farmhands about the crops and animals. When it came time for the spring planting, she learned which fields should remain fallow and which could be cultivated. There was a lot to running the estate, and it kept her busy, but she discovered that she enjoyed it.

Managing the estate left little time for her to take part in the social responsibilities of being a duchess and a lady of the ton, but her family was far more important to her. Besides, Amelia figured, the less she saw of society, the less she would have to explain. By now, she felt that it must be common knowledge that Woodford was no longer staying at Gatewood. Amelia did not want to have to explain the duke's absence and, God forbid, who had to take his place in running the estate. She knew that, in high society, women did not manage the businesses and farms or make financial decisions. That was left for the men to do. And her husband's cruelty was an issue that she did not want any members of the ton to know about. She was aware that the servants of the household would frequently talk to servants from other households, but she hoped they would keep the secrets of Gatewood confidential and not say anything to anyone.

So life went on with Amelia making the decisions that impacted the estate while Woodford went about his own life. Every so often, he would show up for a few hours, look over the books, and then leave again. He simply went into the study and sat at the wide oak desk with the ledgers spread out in front of him. He never asked Amelia to come into the study with him or attempted to talk to her about the figures, but he just sat there and studied what was in front of him. It seemed that he was accepting of the fact that his wife was running the estate and had no desire to change that fact. And to Amelia's delight, the ledgers showed that the farms were showing a profit.

What he didn't know was that Amelia managed to make a few of her own wise investments, separate from those involving the estate, which were proving to be very lucrative. Where Woodford did not have a head for business, Amelia apparently did, and she probably had her father to thank for those genes. She had made the investments as a security blanket, of sorts. If something happened to the estate and their income in the future, at least she would have a sizeable nest egg to fall back on. There was no way of knowing what the future held, but she could at least prepare for it not only for her own sake but also for her children's.

For the last few years, Woodford had felt trapped. He loved his wife and children, but he'd never been able to shake the feeling that something was missing. Since he'd been living at the London townhome, he'd only sunk deeper into his depression. He was angry and drunk most of the time, and the estate seemed to be doing well without any of his input, which only made him feel worse. He knew that Amelia was responsible for its success, which upset him as well. It seemed that he was a failure at everything he touched, so to pass the days, he drank—sometimes at home or other times at the taverns and social clubs throughout London, but always to excess. And in the morning when he awoke with a pounding headache, he'd start all over again. It was a vicious cycle with seemingly no end in sight, but he didn't have the energy to care.

More than once he found himself tangled up in a barroom brawl. He tried to take out his frustrations with his fists, but all that did was give him sore knuckles and usually a bloody lip and a black eye. It just never seemed to get any better, no matter what avenue he took for an escape.

Then late one evening, Woodford had been staggering home from the Hammer and Sickle when a couple of men attacked him. From what he could tell, they seemed to be young, maybe late teens, but very strong. He was no match for them in his drunken state as they beat him up and took his wallet and gold cufflinks. He lay under a gaslight in the filth of the street until he had the energy to pick himself up again and continue his inebriated walk to the townhome. He decided at that point that this was no life for a duke, a husband, or a father, so he needed to start behaving like one. His place was back at Gatewood with Amelia, Herbert, and Charlotte.

Early the next morning, he packed a valise with a few of his belongings and took the carriage to the estate. As he walked in the door of Gatewood Castle, Flanders was there to greet him.

"Good day, Your Grace." Flanders raised an eyebrow when he saw the bruising around Woodford's eye.

"Hello, Flanders. If you would be so kind as to take my bag up to my rooms, I'll be staying here."

Flanders cast him a questioning look but picked up the valise. Woodford walked into the study, thinking he might as well grab a drink to welcome himself home, but as he looked toward the heavy oak desk, he saw Amelia sitting there with the ledgers and papers spread out in front of her. No matter what else he was feeling, he couldn't deny that, even after all these years, she was still a beautiful woman, and he couldn't help but smile at her.

Her gaze fell on him, but he could tell, even from across the room, that her eyes showed no emotion. He realized he had a lot of work to do to repair the damage he caused over the years.

"Hello, Amelia. How are you?" he asked cautiously.

She tipped her head with a frown creasing her brow. "What are you doing here, especially this early in the day?"

"I've come home. I've decided that my place is here at the estate with you and the children." He raised his chin defiantly, expecting her to challenge his decision.

Amelia stood up from the desk and walked out the door without looking back. Woodford hung his head and sighed. He needed that drink.

✍

Over the next few days, Woodford tried to reintroduce himself to the goings-on around the estate. He would ride Pegasus for hours, looking over the land, and he was stunned at how well the farms were doing. The crops were growing very well, and there seemed to be more animals in the fields than ever before. He could clearly see that Amelia had done a fine job managing the estate, but still he felt lost, almost resentful, that she had done so well without him.

He made a point of eating meals with his family, but that proved to be very difficult for everyone. Amelia was hesitant to look at him and did so only when she had to, and the children were very quiet when he was present. The conversations were mostly between Amelia and the children, and if he tried to join in, the conversations abruptly ended. He was a stranger within his own family, and he didn't know how to break the ice.

Within a week or so, all seemed to come to an unspoken understanding. Woodford made no attempt to manage the finances of the estate, so Amelia quietly continued with those duties. The children cautiously accepted him into their lives but were still quite standoffish toward him. They were able to have some small conversations, but that was about it. There were no hugs and kisses at bedtime for their father, only their mother. Woodford would stand back and watch out of the corner of his eyes while his children showered their mother with affection. But when it came to him, they showed him nothing but indifference.

It had been a long time since they had gone out publicly together, but one evening just before dinner, Woodford asked Amelia to go with him to a small card party. Only a few couples had been invited, but at one time, these same couples had all been close friends.

"Lord Thomas is having a small gathering later tonight. I would like it very much if you would go with me."

Amelia hadn't expected this. She straightened her back and placed her hands in her lap, still looking at him. It was a tense moment before she said anything. "I'm not sure that would be a good idea, Woodford. I have no desire to attend any parties."

"I understand, but I would truly be happy if you would come with me. It's been a long time since we've gone out together, and this is only a small gathering of a few couples to play cards."

"But, Woodford, you know how much I dislike your drinking habits. I don't care to witness it firsthand."

"If I promise not to get inebriated, would you come then?" he pleaded.

She hesitated, drawing a deep breath. "Do you truly mean that, Woodford? Can I trust your word?"

"Yes, Amelia, you can trust my word. I would very much like to go with you on my arm. It's been a long time since we've had such fun together."

"I suppose it would be fun. I haven't been out in such a long time, and I do miss our friends. All right, Woodford. I shall go with you." She could feel the corners of her mouth turn up into a smile as she agreed to go, and it felt good to smile at him.

Amelia knew that after being away from the social circuit for so long, it would be very difficult to step back into society, acting as if nothing was wrong. But she decided that if he truly was back in their lives, it would have to happen at some point. Most of her gowns were now outdated, but since this was a small gathering, she figured it wouldn't matter a whole lot. It might not be a bad idea though to invest in a few new gowns, just to have on hand.

When they arrived at the gathering and were announced, she noticed that several of the other guests raised their eyebrows. She forced herself to smile as Woodford took her gently by the arm and led her toward their friends.

"Come, darling. Let's go visit with our host," he prompted.

The evening passed quickly with lots of fun and laughter, and Amelia had felt more comfortable at the party than she thought she would be. Amelia discovered, to her surprise, that she missed her friends even more than she realized.

When they finally left for home, they rode in the carriage with Woodford sitting on one side and Amelia on the bench across from him. The evening was warm, and the moon was shining brightly. He could see that, as she looked out the window, she had a slight smile on her lips, and her eyes seemed to sparkle more than they had in a long while. As the carriage came to a stop in front of Gatewood, Woodford quickly stepped down from the carriage, even before the footman had a chance, and held his hand out to assist her. She looked at him for a moment, hesitating, but then she put her hand in his and stepped down from the carriage.

Once inside, they said good night to each other in the hallway. She went upstairs to her rooms while Woodford headed for the library. Although she noticed that he had a couple of drinks at the party, he had kept his promise and didn't overindulge.

*Maybe he's going to the library for a brandy before bed*, she thought, but she hoped he would leave it alone. It appeared that he'd cut down on the drink lately, and she hoped he would continue to drink less.

As Rose helped Amelia out of her gown, she said, "You seem happier tonight than you have in ages, my lady. You enjoyed the evening?"

"Oh, yes, Rose. It really was a delightful evening. We enjoyed ourselves immensely. And Woodford kept to his promise by not becoming inebriated. It's been a long time since we've enjoyed an evening such as this one. But I must say I felt a bit uncomfortable in this dress since it's a few years out of fashion. I think you and I should go shopping for a few new gowns tomorrow."

"My lady, you know how much I enjoy shopping! It will be a fine way to spend the day!"

Amelia was still too full of energy to sleep, so she turned down the wick on the table lamp but left enough of a flame so she could read a bit before she fell asleep. Before long, her eyelids grew heavy, and she started to doze with the book resting on her lap.

Suddenly a light rapping at the door startled her awake. She hadn't been keeping the door locked since Woodford had moved out, and she suddenly thought how foolish she'd been now that he had returned. The door was still unlocked. Again she heard rapping at the door, a bit louder this time.

*I'm behaving like a scared child,* Amelia thought as she got out of bed, put on her robe, and walked toward the door.

Nonetheless, she cautiously opened the door to find Woodford standing there with a tumbler of amber liquid in his hand. At some point between the library and her chambers, he had taken off his jacket and waistcoat and loosened his silk cravat. Even after all this time, he still made her heart skip a beat when she saw him. There was no denying that he was a good-looking man.

"Can I come in? I'd like to talk to you, if you don't mind." He looked into her eyes.

She hesitated but stepped back to allow him in. She started to close the door but decided against it and left it open a bit. He stood in the middle of the room, waiting for her to make the first move.

She stood firmly by the door. "What did you want to speak to me about?" She raised an eyebrow in a questioning look.

"May I sit down?" He gestured toward one of the overstuffed armchairs in the corner.

She motioned with a sweep of her hand toward the chairs. At least with the door open, if he tried to hit her again or worse, she could scream for help. He sat in one chair; she sat in the other facing him.

"Amelia, I have to be honest with you. I enjoyed your company tonight a great deal. I've missed Herbert and Charlotte and watching them as they grow. But I'm not sure I'm the kind of man you and the children deserve. I'm a very troubled man."

Amelia watched him but never uttered a word. He sat hunched over with his elbows on his knees, staring at the floor. Every once in a while, he took a sip from the glass.

Finally she grew impatient enough to ask, "What is it that you want, Woodford?" There was no hiding the caution in her voice.

"I don't know actually. I would like to stay here at Gatewood, to stay in your life and our children's lives. But I'm no good at running the estate. You have proven yourself worthier than I, and I think it best if you continued in that capacity. I have no business sense and would only run it into the ground." He took another sip from the tumbler.

She didn't say anything for a long moment but kept her eyes on him as if trying to reach into the depths of his heart and mind to see what was there.

Finally she spoke. "I don't expect things will ever be as they once were, but if you wish to stay here at Gatewood, you may. It is your family's estate after all. I would ask, however, that you keep your drinking to a minimum. The children don't need to witness any more of the effects it has on you than they've already seen. In turn, we can continue to attend the various social functions as husband and wife, but that's where the marital relationship ends. Your rooms are as you left them. They have not been touched."

He nodded his head, acknowledging the agreement, and left Amelia's room, closing the door behind him. She sat in the chair for a long time before finally giving a long, cleansing sigh and going back to bed. Only time would tell if this arrangement were going to work.

Amelia strolled through the garden, taking a few quiet moments to herself. She thought back on the last six months since Woodford's return. She sighed, feeling the weight of the world on her shoulders. She and her husband had gone to a few parties and social events, but not many. And true to his word, he had left the business end of things to Amelia's care, but that was the only promise he kept.

He still drank a great deal and would very often have terrible fits of anger. There was no telling what would set him off or what to expect when it happened. The children tried hard to stay out of his way, but when their paths did cross, he had harsh words for them. Amelia was constantly on edge, trying to listen for any raised voices so she could defuse any potential problems. Unfortunately that didn't always work if she were in a different part of the home. Without her around to stop him, he would grab the children by the shoulders and shake them, leaving them dizzy and scared. He screamed at them about the most nonsensical things—if there was a spot of dirt on their clothes, if they came in from a rainstorm and dripped water onto the floor, or if they were playing too loudly and disturbed him. He had become a tinderbox with a very short fuse.

Herbert, now ten years old, would stand up to his father and try not to let his fear show. He would raise his chin and look his father in the eye, knowing he was about to feel the elder man's wrath, but he wouldn't back down. He was trying to be a man, and Amelia's heart ached for him. *He shouldn't have to grow up so fast when he is still so young.*

Charlotte tended to stay in her room when she wasn't with her mother, Rose, or Mrs. Parker. If Charlotte knew her father was home but needed to leave her room, she crept cautiously down the halls, peeking around the corners until she reached her destination. At only five years old, she had figured out that it was the safest thing to do when her father might be around.

Rose found herself at the receiving end of the duke's temper one morning when she met him in the downstairs hallway.

Woodford walked toward her but stopped in front of her, blocking her path. "What are you doing?" he yelled at Rose.

Amelia had been working in the study when she heard her husband's yelling. She rushed into the hall in time to see him swing at the tea tray Rose was carrying, sending it crashing to the floor. Before Amelia could do anything, Woodford pushed Rose on both shoulders hard enough that she fell backward and landed on the floor with a sickening thud.

Amelia quickly ran toward them, putting herself between Rose and Woodford. "Woodford, stop! What do you think you're doing?" Amelia knelt next to Rose.

Woodford kicked a teacup and sent it sailing across the marble floor. It shattered as it smashed into the wall. Amelia saw the anger in her husband's eyes before he spun on his heel and walked up the stairs.

"Rose, are you all right?" she asked. "Are you hurt?"

"It's my head, my lady. I hit the back of my head when I fell to the floor." Rose put her hand to her head as the tears fell from her eyes.

"It's all right, Rose. We'll send for Dr. Kerr to come take a look at you. Let's get you to your room."

An unusually warm spring afternoon at the end of April found Amelia walking in the gardens. It felt wonderful to be outside after having been cooped up for most of the winter. With a sigh, Amelia went back in the house. She had some work to do, and it wasn't going to get done with her whiling away the day by meandering through the gardens.

As soon as she went to the study, she had Rose open the windows and pull back the heavy draperies so she could enjoy the gentle breeze as she pored over the books of the estate. She loved the spring air when it smelled so crisp and fresh.

"My lady, would you like some hibiscus tea? And I believe Cook made some fresh tarts this morning, if you'd like."

"That sounds wonderful, Rose. Thank you."

A few minutes later, Rose was bringing the tea to Amelia when both turned toward the door as they realized that Woodford had followed Rose into the study. The maid glanced over her shoulder at him as she set down the tray. With a slight nod of Amelia's head, Rose was granted permission to leave. Rose gave a quick curtsy and whisked out the door past Woodford, with one hand clasping her cameo brooch and her eyes downcast.

Woodford stood boldly in front of Amelia, who was still sitting at the desk with a pen in hand, trying to maintain her composure. "I'd like to see the books," he demanded.

Amelia looked up at him and noticed the glass in his hand. She studied his eyes to determine how much he'd had to drink. Judging by the redness, she guessed quite a bit.

"That's fine. What would you like to see?" She set the pen down on the desk.

"All of it. I want to know how much I'm worth." He reached across the desk and pulled one of the ledgers away from Amelia, almost spilling the inkwell.

"You won't find much about your worth in that book. I keep track of the livestock on the farm in that one."

He threw the book at her. "Well, which one is it? Which is the financial ledger? I want to see it now!"

Amelia bit her cheek to keep from saying something she might regret. Letting him see that she was getting angry only made things worse, so she fought to control her own emotions. She found the correct ledger and handed it to him. He snatched it out of her hand and walked over to one of the chairs across the room. He set his drink on the side table and began to turn the pages of the book. Knowing he wasn't good with numbers, she had no idea how much information he would gather from the columns, but he did seem to be looking at them.

Amelia picked up one of the other ledgers, but she couldn't fully comprehend the pages in front of her. Her mind was on her husband, who sat across the room, thumbing through the ledger. She tried to discreetly watch him out of the corner of her eye. He was turning the pages so quickly that Amelia would wager that he wasn't even reading the entries. She figured he might as well have been reading the ledger upside down for all that he was gleaning from it. *What is he doing? Woodford has said many times that he doesn't care to look at the books. What is he looking for?*

After only a moment, Woodford crossed the room and tossed the ledger on the desk. It slid across the waxed oak surface, almost landing in Amelia's lap. "Is that it? Where are the rest of the assets? There has to be more than that!" he bellowed.

Amelia tried to remain calm while she talked with her husband. There was no point in getting as angry as he was. "I'm sure you understand that the cash accounts are a bit lower momentarily because we had to make some purchases for the spring planting. Rest assured the cash on hand will improve substantially after harvest and after some of the sheep and pigs are sold."

She'd never told him about the personal investments she'd made and certainly had no intention of telling him now. That information was logged in a separate set of books that she kept hidden in a secret safe she'd had installed behind one of the paintings on the wall. Only she and Flanders knew the combination to the safe.

"Why are you asking? It was my understanding that the management of the estate's finances would be left to my care. Are you in need of money?" She fought to control the shaking she could hear in her own voice.

He dropped his voice but spoke through clenched teeth. "I shouldn't have to ask my wife for money. It isn't proper, and I won't do it. I will be handling the accounts from now on."

Amelia could see the redness in his cheeks and knew he was getting very angry. She stood up to confront him while still trying to maintain her composure. "I thought we had an understanding. Because you're not fond of bookkeeping, I was to be the one to take care of the finances."

"This land is mine! It belonged to my father and his father before him for many generations! I will see to it from now on. Not you! I am the man of the home. Do you hear me?" He was so close to her that she could see his spittle flying through the air as he yelled.

Before she knew what was happening, Amelia felt the sting of his slap on her cheek. She fell to the floor, hitting her head on the corner of the desk on the way down. As she lay crumpled on the floor, her hand went to the side of her head, and she felt the wet stickiness of blood. He was around the desk and straddling her in an instant, wrapping both hands around her neck, choking her. She saw stars as she struggled to breathe, but his grip was tightening around her throat.

She tried to yell, but nothing came out. Suddenly he was off her, almost flying, and she gasped for precious air. She looked up in time to see Flanders and Parker dragging her husband away from her, out the door and into the hallway. Each had a firm hold of him by the upper arms, and his feet were scrambling along the floor in a vain attempt to right himself. He continued to yell and kept trying to pull away, but they held on tightly to him.

Rose ran into the study after hearing the commotion and found her mistress on the floor, holding her throat and bleeding from the gash on her head.

"Oh! My lady! What happened?" Rose knelt and dabbed at Amelia's bleeding scalp with her apron.

Amelia was too stunned to talk as she gulped for air and tears fell down her cheeks.

# Chapter 6

Amelia's head throbbed as she pulled herself up on her feet, using the desk as leverage. She heard Flanders and Parker yelling at Woodford and then the heavy thud of footsteps growing fainter as the seconds passed. She felt the hot sting of tears on her cheeks.

"Are you okay, my lady?" Rose asked.

Flanders and Parker entered the study.

"Is he gone?" she asked Flanders.

Flanders nodded. "For now, my lady. Are you all right?" He looked at her with concern.

"Oh, Flanders, I don't understand this. What causes him to be so angry?" She was wringing her hands so hard that her knuckles were turning white.

Flanders hesitated, finally saying, "Ma'am, I wish I knew. He's always had a temper, but it seems worse than ever before, especially when he's been imbibing in the drink. Regardless of the reason, there's no excuse for what he's done. If you don't mind me being so forward, my lady, I will do whatever it takes to protect you."

"Thank you."

Rose came back with a bowl of water and fresh bandages. Amelia's head was spinning, but she tried her best to sit still long enough for Rose to dress the wound and wrap the bandage around her head. When Rose was finished, Amelia went up to her room, with Rose promising to bring her a tray of tea and broth right away.

An hour later, Mrs. Parker left after finishing the day's lessons. Herbert and Charlotte came bounding in to Amelia's room. They apparently had not heard the commotion going on downstairs, for which Amelia was grateful. Charlotte climbed on the bed to snuggle with Amelia, but Herbert stopped dead in his tracks when he saw the bandage wrapped around his mother's head. Amelia watched as his smile faded and the color drained from his face.

Charlotte spoke first. "What happened to your head, Mother? That's a silly hat you're wearing."

"I just had a little accident is all. I was being clumsy and careless. Why don't you and Herbert go down to the kitchen to see if Cook will give you a snack?"

"All right, Mother!" Charlotte scrambled off the bed and skipped out the door, singing a nursery rhyme to herself as she went.

"Mother," Herbert said carefully, "what really happened?" He remained rooted to the spot.

Amelia wasn't sure how to answer her son's question. She could tell that he wasn't falling for the fib she told Charlotte. *How much should I tell him?*

Herbert tipped his head and coolly asked, "Where is Father?"

Amelia could see the anger burning in his eyes. She took a deep breath and winced, only aggravating the pounding in her head. "I don't know. He left on horseback." She brought her hand up to the bandage.

He kept his eyes locked on hers before finally turning on his heel and leaving his mother's room. Herbert was going on eleven years old now, but Amelia just watched as her son aged beyond his years right before her eyes.

∽◊

Woodford returned later that night, so drunk he was barely able to sit atop Pegasus. Parker and one of the groomsmen met him as he rode up to the stables. They held on to Pegasus's reins to try to steady the horse while Woodford all but fell out of the saddle.

"Let's see if he can find his own way back to the manor house," Parker said to the groomsman at his side. "I'll not help him. With luck, he'll fall into the bushes and spend the night with the rest of the worms."

For the next few days, Amelia stayed in her chambers. Every time she attempted to stand up, she'd see stars, so until that passed, she was better off staying in bed. Dr. Kerr had been in to see her every day and would check her head and change the bandages. He was prescribing laudanum to help with the pain, but Amelia only took it at night when the household was asleep. Under the circumstances, she felt she needed to stay alert and aware of the goings-on in her home, even with the constant drumming in her head that made so many things difficult to do.

"I will never again take for granted the ability to sit up without seeing stars or being able to walk without feeling light-headed," she confided to Rose.

Rose stayed by Amelia's side throughout the days and nights while Mrs. Parker remained with the children during the day. The children came in to visit their mother as often as they could, but Amelia felt it was important they keep to their daily schedule for normalcy's sake. Maintaining their routine would help maintain a bit of order in their young lives, so Mrs. Parker continued with their lessons.

Amelia noticed that Flanders and Parker always seemed to be sticking close to her and the children, especially when Woodford was somewhere on the estate. Their presence, loyalty, and protection comforted her.

Woodford remained in the home but spent most of his time in the study with the ledgers and the alcohol as his companions, although as far as Amelia could tell, he rarely touched one but constantly imbibed in the other. When he did leave the study, it was to go into London to spend hours on end at the Hammer and Sickle.

Once she was feeling better, Amelia ventured into the study, but only after Flanders assured her that Woodford had left. Having a chance meeting with him was something that Amelia was determined to avoid. He must have known that she was still managing the finances for the estate because he would have seen the notations in the ledgers, but he never said anything to her. And for that, Amelia was grateful.

The summer months had been very dry. The animals had enough water, thanks to the creek that ran through the estate, but the crops were suffering. When possible, the farmhands were carrying water in buckets from the creek to the fields, but it was slow, tedious work. No sooner had they watered all the crops when they had to go back to the beginning and do it all over again. The hands worked on this routine two or three times a week, with each complete pass taking about two days.

Amelia would ride out to the farms every couple of days and was brokenhearted to see the crops in such bad shape, but she also knew that this was life on a farmed estate. It would mean buying hay and corn from neighboring estates to feed the animals during the winter months, but there was enough money in the coffers for just such a circumstance. Amelia had planned and planned well, knowing that losing the crops was always a concern for a farmed estate.

Amelia was in the study one fall afternoon discussing her plans with Parker to buy additional feed. He had become as much of a trusted employee as his wife, and Amelia leaned on them both quite heavily.

He was able to offer a possible solution. "I believe Mr. Fitzpatrick down the road has extra hay that he might sell, and Mr. Johns has already agreed to sell us whatever extra corn he has available. I believe, with what we purchase along with what has survived in our fields, we should be able to make it through the winter months, if we're careful."

"That's wonderful news, Mr. Parker. I'm grateful that we have such helpful neighbors."

The heavy door to the study flew open and banged against the wall. Woodford stood there glaring at them, his face flushed with anger. *Or is he flushed from the whiskey?* Amelia pondered.

"What, may I ask, is going on in here?" Woodford thundered.

Parker turned around to face Woodford, not sure what His Grace was implying.

"We are making arrangements to buy additional feed for the animals that will see us through the winter months," Amelia answered coolly. She remained seated behind the desk while Parker stood in front of her, angrily fidgeting with the cap he carried in his hands.

"And how do you anticipate doing that?"

"Woodford, if you'd like to discuss this with us, you're more than welcome to, but if you're going to continue to raise your voice, I would ask that you come back when you're in a calmer frame of mind." She almost sounded to her own ears like she was speaking to the children when they were younger, but the truth of the matter was that she truly didn't care anymore how she sounded to him.

Woodford took two steps into the study, but that was as far as he got before Parker stood in front of him, blocking his way further into the room.

"You heard her, Your Grace, sir. You'll have to come back at another time."

"So that's how it is, eh, Amelia?" Woodford looked over Parker's shoulder at Amelia. "You've got Parker to protect you now? Is he keeping you warm at night too?"

Amelia sat at the desk, her breath quickening and her hands clasped together in front of her so tightly that her fingernails dug into her hands, leaving crescent-shaped marks. But she wouldn't rise to the bait and comment on his accusations. She glared at Woodford, angered by not only his actions but also his verbal assault.

Woodford glanced from Amelia to Parker and back again before he turned and stormed out. They heard the front door slam, and both breathed a sigh of relief.

"I'm sorry, Mr. Parker. I'm sorry you had to witness such an outburst. He doesn't know what he's saying."

"I understand, Your Grace. It isn't him that's talking. It's the drink."

Amelia blinked back the tears that were filling her eyes. "I think that's enough for now, Mr. Parker. We'll go ahead with the plans we've discussed for the feed, if you'd like to make the arrangements." Her voice was shaking, and her shoulders slumped forward as she spoke.

"Yes, ma'am. I'll see to it right away." He looked at Amelia as if there were more that he wanted to say, but thankfully, he just turned and left.

As Parker shut the door behind him, Amelia put her head in her hands and quietly cried.

While the summer had been very warm and dry, the winter was unseasonably cold and snowy, but Amelia and the children made the most of it. They would bundle up under warm blankets and go on long carriage rides across the estate. Then as soon as they got back, Charlotte would scurry into the kitchen to ask Cook to fix some of her special hot cocoa for them.

And when the weather was good enough to travel, they would take a carriage into London to shop and ice-skate. (Their own creek was too shallow and rocky to skate on.) Charlotte was still learning how to skate, but Herbert proved to be very good at it and would literally skate in circles around his mother and sister, to their delight.

The Christmas holiday was a time that Amelia wanted to make especially festive at Gatewood. She and the children made decorations to hang on the Christmas tree, and she had them loop fresh evergreen boughs and red ribbon along the banister of the grand staircase. When Cook made fruitcakes, puddings, and cookies, they helped with that too, although their way of helping consisted mostly of sampling the baked goods.

Christmas morning arrived, and after going to mass at the chapel on the estate, the family went back to Gatewood for a breakfast celebration. Woodford had stayed at Gatewood, choosing not to go to mass, but he did join the family for breakfast. He seemed to be in better spirits than he had been in for quite a while.

After breakfast, when it came time to open the gifts, they went to the grand dining hall, family and staff alike. The tree was glowing brightly with all the lit candles that adorned the branches as the Yule log burned in the fireplace. The gifts under the tree were wrapped in beautiful papers and ribbons, making the scene as beautiful as Amelia could have hoped for, but she only had a few moments to admire their hard work.

A very impatient Herbert and Charlotte were too excited to wait any longer and started passing out the gifts, while the adults took their seats. As the children unwrapped their own gifts, their faces would light up in delight at each surprise. Apples and oranges filled their stockings, and both were given new winter coats. Herbert received new ice skates, while Charlotte was given a new porcelain doll. It was wonderful to see the children so happy.

With Mrs. Parker's help, the children had purchased a gift for both their mother and their father on one of the outings to London. They gave Amelia a beautiful gold bracelet with a cloisonné pendant on the top.

"I will cherish it forever," she proudly told them as she placed it around her wrist.

Herbert found the gift that had their father's name on it and hesitantly handed it to him, but not before Amelia noticed the look on her son's face. His eyes were downcast, and his lips were set in a tight line, almost as if he detested being near his father. She hoped she had misinterpreted his expression, but something told her she had not.

Woodford opened the box and stared down at the gift for what seemed like a long time. The children had picked out a gold stickpin with a large piece of amber at its tip that he could wear in his cravat. For a moment, Amelia wasn't sure why he had that reaction or what he was going to do.

Finally he looked up. "Thank you, Herbert. Thank you, Charlotte. It truly is lovely." He cast a sideways glance at Amelia.

She held his gaze and smiled at him. He smiled back. At least for one day, they could let bygones be bygones and try to be a happy family.

But just when they thought the gift giving was over, Rose and Flanders came in, each with a small bundle in their arms. The children looked up, wide-eyed, with their mouths forming small Os as they realized what Rose and Flanders had.

Rose walked toward Charlotte and put a tiny kitten in her arms while Flanders gave Herbert a puppy. Both children squealed with delight as they hugged their new pets.

"Oh, Mother, look at this cute little kitty! She's beautiful!" Charlotte ran to Amelia and then Rose, carefully giving each a hug while still clutching the all-white kitten that wore a bright pink ribbon around her neck.

Herbert held the puppy, a black and white border collie that was giving him wet kisses on his nose, and laughed. "I've always wanted a puppy! Thank you, Rose! Thank you, Mr. Flanders!"

"You'll have to think of good names for them," their father instructed.

But the children were too busy with their new pets to pay attention to their father.

# Chapter 7

The rest of the winter season passed without incident. Finally the cold and snow gave way to warmer weather and spring flowers. The staff was busy opening windows and cleaning Gatewood, giving the manor a fresh and airy feel.

Herbert and the puppy had become inseparable. They slept, studied, and played together, but because of the trouble the collie always seemed to find, Herbert had named the dog Mayhem. He constantly tripped over his own feet, and his long, furry tail always seemed to slap at Herbert and anything else that was in its path.

During lessons with Mrs. Parker, Herbert tried desperately to keep the puppy quiet, but Mayhem had other ideas. He would nudge Herbert's elbow, causing the pen to skip across the paper, leaving streaks of black ink. Other times, he would put his front paws on the table next to his young master and knock the books and papers to the floor. But Mayhem's favorite trick was to nibble at Herbert's feet so he would have a hard time concentrating on his lessons.

Eventually Mayhem would tire himself out and take a nap so Mrs. Parker would be able to teach uninterrupted. Mayhem was undoubtedly a test for Mrs. Parker's patience, but she didn't mind.

The puppy was playful and mischievous, but he put a smile on Herbert's face, and Lord knows, he could have used all the smiles he could get.

Charlotte named her kitten Honeysuckle after her favorite flower and would put a fresh colorful ribbon around the kitten's neck every day. They would also spend most of their time together, but in true cat fashion, Honeysuckle would venture throughout the castle on occasion in search of mice, spiders, or anything else that she could hunt.

Woodford did not appear to be drinking as much in the past few months; however, Amelia reserved judgment on that fact. She'd seen it before where he would go a period of time without drinking to excess, but then he would start up again and fall right back into his bad habits. And frankly she didn't trust him. Now that the roads were passable, he just might be itching to get out and about, to frequent the taverns again.

One particularly warm morning in early March, Woodford had ridden off on Pegasus. Amelia hoped he was going to inspect the fields of the estate, but something deep inside told her that wasn't the case. Her fear was confirmed later that evening when he returned very much in his cups. He led Pegasus to the stables and left Parker to take care of the horse while he stumbled toward the house.

Amelia had been working on her needlepoint in the parlor when she heard him yelling for Flanders while he was still outdoors. She walked into the hallway to see Flanders holding the door open. When Woodford staggered in, Flanders just stepped aside. There was no hat for Flanders to take. It had been lost somewhere, probably on the journey home. So he simply helped His Grace shrug out of his coat.

"Woodford, how nice to see you." Amelia could hear the contempt in her own voice.

"What are you looking at, woman? Go about your business

and leave me alone. Haven't you got anything better to do than stare at me?"

Amelia chose to remain quiet rather than take the bait. She had enjoyed a nice, quiet spring day and would rather not see it end by having an argument with her husband. She simply stood in the doorway to the parlor with her hands clenched tightly together at her waist.

She watched with a sickening knot in her stomach as her husband staggered toward the stairs to find his way to his chambers. He stopped and looked up. Herbert and Mayhem were standing between him and the stairs. Mayhem stood in front of Herbert in a protective stance with his eyes on the elder man and the hair on his back raised. Herbert stood there with a look of utter disgust on his face.

As the duke passed in front of them, he looked at his son, slurring, "What is the problem, son?"

Herbert didn't answer him, but Mayhem let out a low growl. The duke tried to focus his glazed-over eyes on the dog. Suddenly he kicked at Mayhem, hitting him square in the ribs. Before the boy could react, Mayhem latched onto the duke's leg with tightly clenched teeth, pulling and shaking the limb as if it were a piece of rope he was playing tug-of-war with.

The duke was yelling, "Get him off me! Get that bloody dog off me!"

As the elder man kicked his leg, trying to loosen the dog, he fell to the floor. It was only then that the dog released his bite but continued to bark and growl at the duke.

Amelia had stepped further into the hallway as the scene unfolded around her, yelling, "Herbert! Get the dog and take him outside."

Herbert obeyed, grabbed the dog's collar, and walked him outside without ever looking back at his father lying sprawled on the floor. The duke struggled to get up, but between the slippery marble floor, the alcohol, and the bite on his leg, he was having trouble getting to his feet. Flanders managed to help him stand and led him to one of the chairs in the hallway.

A bit of blood was already soaking through his torn pant leg, but from a distance, Amelia didn't think it appeared to be that bad. She figured that a bit of cleaning and a bandage should take care of it, but she would leave it to Flanders. She had no desire to nurse her husband's injury.

The following day, Amelia had been working in the study with the window open when she heard Woodford shouting to have Pegasus saddled up for a ride into town. She stood watching from the window and could tell by his demeanor that he must still be angry at the world. She could see one of the young stable hands cinching up the saddle belt when Woodford reached over and pushed the boy out of the way.

"Get out of my bloody way. I'll do it myself, you good-for-nothing—"

She didn't hear him finish his sentence, but it didn't matter. The stable hand stepped back. Amelia could see Pegasus shifting from one foot to the next, as if he could sense the tension in the air, which only made it more difficult for her husband to tighten the saddle.

"Stand still, you filthy animal!" he yelled.

Woodford landed a punch on the horse's flank, and Pegasus tossed his head in surprise. He was finally able to secure the saddle, mount the horse, and race out of the barn. He slapped the reins back and forth over Pegasus's shoulders, trying to get the mount to move faster and faster. Pegasus responded and cantered down the road with his head held tight from the reins.

Amelia turned back to the desk, shaking her head in disbelief.

A week later, Herbert Woodford, Duke of Brazelton was dead. One of the maids found him after she knocked on the door of the study, and when no one answered, she went in. She saw his body lying next to the desk with a large, bloody gash on his head and a pool of blood on the carpet. Next to him on the floor was a brass bookend in the shape of an elephant, its trunk pointing upward in the traditional show of good luck.

She let out a bloodcurdling scream that brought everyone in the house scurrying toward the study. Flanders was the first one to reach her as she stood locked in place, making a whimpering sound and staring at the grisly scene. When he saw the body and the blood, he grabbed the maid's shoulders, gently turning her away. He was careful to shut the door to the study behind him and led the maid into the hall where other members of the staff had started to gather.

All seemed to be talking at once.

"What happened?"

"What's going on?"

"Who screamed?"

Flanders pushed through the growing crowd to lead the frightened and shaking maid toward Rose, who had only just arrived.

"Rose," he pleaded, "please tend to her. I'll be right back." As an afterthought, he added, "Don't let anyone go in that room."

Flanders looked over the heads of the staff in search of Amelia. She had seen him first and rushed toward him, pushing past the servants that had gathered. He stepped outside the circle of people and cut her off before she could get any closer to the study.

"Flanders, what's going on? I thought I heard someone scream." Amelia looked around, trying to make sense of the scene surrounding her.

But everyone was talking at once, eyes opened wide in a show of confusion, and none of it made sense to her.

"My lady, come with me, please." He touched her elbow and led her to the side, nearer the wall. He spoke as gently and quietly as he could so the others did not hear him. "Your Grace, I'm so sorry to tell you this. Someone has attacked the duke in the study. He is dead."

She stood there staring at him, open-mouthed, and then swooned as the realization of what he said sunk in. Flanders reached out to guide Amelia toward a bench and helped her to sit down. She could hardly breathe after hearing the news. The world started to close in on her as the blood drained from her face and dark shadows clouded her vision.

"He's dead? My husband is dead?" she asked in disbelief. She looked at Flanders and tipped her head to the side, as if he were speaking in a foreign language.

"Yes, Your Grace, he is gone."

"I don't understand. How can that be?" Amelia attempted to stand, but her knees were too weak to support her, and she collapsed onto the bench.

Flanders called for one of the maids to bring Amelia a glass of water. She took the glass filled with cold water but just looked at it, as if it were a foreign object that she didn't know what to do with it.

"Your Grace, take a sip of water. Please." Flanders guided the hand that was holding the glass toward her lips. She instinctively took a sip but wasn't aware that she'd done it.

After a few moments, Amelia squared her shoulders and took a deep breath. "Flanders, what happened to my husband? What do you mean *he was attacked?*"

Amelia noticed how he hesitated. "It appears that he was hit over the head while he was in the study this morning. The maid has just now found him lying on the floor."

"We'll need to notify the police. Would you do that for me, Flanders?" she asked weakly.

"Of course, Your Grace. I will see to it that someone fetches the doctor as well."

Suddenly Amelia looked at Flanders in horror. "What will I tell the children? How do I tell them that their father is dead? Oh, Flanders, I'll have to tell them right away. I don't want them to hear this terrible news from someone else. I should be the one to tell them. Flanders, will you inform the staff? They will need to know as well. I need to stay here for a moment to get my wits about me, and then I will go to the children."

Flanders turned around to face the staff. "If I could have your attention, please. I have some terrible news. The duke has been found dead in the study."

There was a collective gasp at his announcement. Parker had just arrived when Flanders turned to him. "Parker, I'll ask you to stand guard at the door to the study so no one enters." Flanders then turned to one of the footmen. "I need you to get the doctor and the police as quickly as you can."

A couple of the maids started to cry, but most of the staff just stared wide-eyed, their glances bouncing between each other and Amelia.

"You all have something that needs doing, so I suggest you return to your work," Flanders gently coaxed them.

They broke into small groups and headed in different directions, all the while speaking with each other in hushed voices.

"Thank you, Flanders. I must go to the children now."

Amelia struggled to gather as much energy as she could to lift herself up from the bench and walk upstairs, each step heavier than the last. She hung onto the railing, fearing that if she let go she would surely collapse. She needed to talk to Herbert and Charlotte, but she didn't know quite how she would tell them or how much they would understand. Neither one had experienced the death of someone so close to them, and having to explain death to her young children was not something that Amelia was looking forward to. Herbert had been only one year old when Amelia's mother passed away, so he would have no memory of that time. Both had been fond of a few of the farm animals that had occasionally passed away, but they were simply told that the animals went to live on another farm.

When she reached the top of the stairs, she took a few moments to compose herself. She needed to be strong. She was not sure who or when, but someone had pressed a lace handkerchief into her hand, and she still gripped it tightly.

*It must have been Flanders*, she thought, although she had no recollection of that happening. She wiped the tears from her eyes with the handkerchief, took a deep breath, and walked toward the nursery.

She opened the nursery door to find Mrs. Parker sitting with both children at the table, absorbed in their studies. Mrs. Parker looked up with a smile, but after seeing the look on Amelia's face, she stood up.

A look of alarm replaced the smile. "Your Grace, what's wrong?"

"Mrs. Parker, if you would please leave me alone with the children, I need to speak to them. But please find Flanders, and he will explain everything."

"Certainly, Your Grace. As you wish." Mrs. Parker quickly gathered her wrap and reticule, gave a small curtsy, and left the room, softly closing the door behind her.

Amelia sat at the table in the chair that Mrs. Parker had just vacated, with her children sitting across from her. She hesitated for just a moment, smoothing out her dress, needing that time to compose herself before she could look at the children.

"Mother, what is it?" Charlotte was growing up to be such a pretty young girl. She had dark, wavy hair so much like her father's.

Herbert, on the other hand, had Amelia's features, dark piercing eyes, and auburn hair that always seemed to hang in his eyes. He was forever pushing it back off his forehead.

She spoke very softly. "I have some terrible news for you, my loves. Your father has had an accident. He's gone. He has died." She couldn't bring herself to tell them the details, that he'd been murdered, killed in their own home.

Charlotte, at six years old, had a limited understanding of the loss but enough to know that her father was gone. She started crying. She scrambled onto Amelia's lap and buried her head and tears in her mother's shoulder. Amelia rubbed her back and made shushing noises, trying to console her daughter.

Herbert just sat there stone-faced. "What happened to him, Mother?"

Amelia knew the question would be coming but hadn't been able to formulate a proper answer for him. Charlotte was too young to understand, but Herbert was an entirely different matter. He was very smart for his age. He was growing up too fast, and as a result, he tended to be precocious.

She met his gaze and knew she had to tell him the truth. "Charlotte, if you would go to your room, please, I'd like to talk to your brother. I'll arrange for some tea to be brought up, and maybe Cook will have one of your favorite tarts for you. Go ahead, and I'll be there in a few minutes."

Charlotte scrambled down from Amelia's lap and wiped her tears with the back of her hands. "All right, Mother."

Amelia used the bellpull to summon a maid and asked for a tea tray to be brought to her daughter's room.

Now it was time to talk to Herbert. "It happened sometime this morning while he was in the study. From what I understand, he was hit over the head with an object. He was murdered."

"Who is responsible?" he asked quietly. Herbert seemed very composed under the circumstances.

"We don't yet know. The police have been called, and they will be investigating."

Herbert turned and calmly walked out of the nursery, leaving Amelia to herself. She stared at the open door that he had just passed through, wondering what her son was thinking. He had been the recipient of his father's angry outbursts more than anyone else, but the duke was, after all, his father.

*What is Herbert feeling? Will he experience a sense of loss for his father? Or is he so angry that he won't feel that loss?* She wished she could tell, but he was unreadable. He seemed so emotionally detached at the news that his father was dead. But Amelia hadn't had time to digest the news herself, and she knew she would have to do that before she could help her children.

# Chapter 8

After Dr. Kerr arrived, he was shown into the study. He carefully checked the duke's body for a pulse, but he knew it was a futile effort. There was no question that the duke was dead.

He returned to the foyer just as the police arrived and put his hand out to the larger of the two officers. "Inspector Duffy, how are you?"

Senior Inspector Patrick Duffy took Dr. Kerr's hand and gave him a firm handshake. The two men had known and worked with each other for many years. "Very good, sir. And yourself?"

"Better than the duke, I must say," the doctor answered bluntly. As he shook hands with Duffy, he felt very confident in the man's ability to get to the bottom of things.

Duffy, a well-respected member of the police department, had joined the force as a young man of twenty years of age, but in all this time, he'd never married. Over the next twenty-two years, he worked his way through the ranks by sheer skill and thoroughness. He loved his job and was obviously very good at it.

Dr. Kerr held his hand out to the second inspector and shook his hand as well. "Inspector Shaw, it's good to see you again."

Inspector Henry Shaw, at twenty-seven years of age, had a

lovely wife at home and two young children. He seemed to have a keen sense for police work and had a good track record for solving crimes. Because of that, he had also risen through the ranks quickly.

Not being one to spend time with social niceties, Inspector Shaw got right to the point. "What do we have, Doctor?"

"It appears the duke has been dead for a few hours, judging by the amount of dried blood, although it doesn't appear that rigor mortis has fully set in. He has a large wound toward the back of his head, and a heavy bookend is next to his body. There appears to be blood on the bookend." Dr. Kerr was careful to give the facts as he saw them rather than any opinions. He would leave the deductions to the investigators.

"Let's go have a look," Shaw prompted.

The two inspectors and Dr. Kerr entered the study slowly and carefully. Before approaching the body, the men scanned the room for any bits of information that might help them figure out who murdered the duke. Dr. Kerr looked at the scene through a medical perspective, while the inspectors viewed the scene from a criminal's view. By working together and yet from different angles, their combined efforts would hopefully lead them to the murderer. It was obvious, after all, that it was indeed a murder.

They moved toward the body and the brass elephant bookend that was lying on the floor next to the duke.

Dr. Kerr pointed to the bookend. "If you look closely, you'll see there is blood and a bit of hair on it. This most definitely is the murder weapon. And the mate to the bookend is still perched on the bookshelf directly behind the desk."

"I would say this means that the murderer had taken one of the bookends from the shelf and hit the duke on the back of the head with it. But why would the duke just sit there while the killer approached and walked behind him?" Shaw asked.

"It almost certainly meant that the killer was someone he knew, maybe even trusted, but wasn't paying too much attention to," answered Duffy.

Duffy and Shaw began looking over the crime scene, making notations in their notepads, and occasionally taking a few items as evidence that they thought might be important, including the pair of bookends. These would be kept until later when they could have a much closer look at each one to see if there were any link between it and the murder.

"This is strange," commented Dr. Kerr. "It looks like a small pearl lying on the duke's back."

Duffy looked closer to where the doctor was pointing. "Hmm. That is strange. It would have to have landed there after he fell to the floor. If it were there before the murder, it would have been on the floor under him. We'll keep this as evidence."

Inspector Shaw looked at the ledgers that lie opened across the top of the desk. "Dr. Kerr, what do you make of this?"

Dr. Kerr looked at the ledgers and began to explain. "Do you see how the blood droplets seem to get narrower at the end? That tail, if you will, points to the direction of travel. In other words, the droplets point away from the chair the duke was sitting on. There's no doubt in my mind that the blood splattered across the ledgers and desktop meant that the duke had been sitting at the desk when he was struck with the bookend."

In looking carefully at the entries in the ledgers, they noticed that nothing seemed to be out of the ordinary in that they were typical ledgers kept by an estate. Figures stacked neatly in columns explained the expenditures, assets, and profits of the farms. They did notice, however, two different styles of handwriting in the ledgers, one being very neat and legible while the other was sloppy and hard to decipher. Shaw made a note to ask Amelia about who was doing the bookkeeping.

"I doubt he was killed over a gambling debt or any of the like," speculated Duffy. "It appeared that the estate was worth a considerable sum with a large amount of available cash, so if the duke owed any debts, he should have been able to cover them."

It had been a long day, and his contribution toward the inspection of the body and the murder scene was done, as far as Dr. Kerr was concerned.

"Gentlemen, if you'll excuse me, I believe I've concluded my assessment of the scene. I will bid you good day. Rose, would you extend my condolences again to Her Grace? She needs her rest, and I don't wish to disturb her."

✍

Before they left, Duffy and Shaw met with Amelia in the parlor to offer their condolences. She tried hard to compose herself, but the shock of it all was weighing her down. She was still clutching the handkerchief, wringing it tightly between her fingers. She found that she couldn't put it down. It was a way to keep her hands busy, though it did nothing to quiet the jumble of thoughts that kept bouncing through her mind.

"Gentlemen, what can you tell me about my husband's murder? Do you know who might have done this?"

Duffy spoke. "Not as yet, Your Grace. A dozen staff members had been working in the house this morning, so Shaw and I split up so we might talk to each person. He and I will compare notes later, but for now, it looks like every one of them had an alibi and could account for their whereabouts during the time when the murder was thought to have taken place. No one had seen or heard anything out of the ordinary, and from what the footmen and Flanders had said, no one had come to the home this morning for a visit or to make deliveries to the kitchen."

"Your Grace," Duffy said as he gently held her hand, "rest

assured that we will do our very best to find out who committed this terrible crime."

"Thank you, Inspector. I have every confidence that you will." Amelia noticed that he never took his eyes off hers and seemed genuine when he spoke to her. She felt confident that he would work very hard to find out who murdered her husband.

"You might consider staying elsewhere for a few days," offered Shaw.

She tipped her chin up a little higher. "I thank you for your concern, Inspector, but we will be fine. I truly don't believe anyone else is in danger. You see, my husband had a vicious temper, and I have to believe that is what brought about his demise." She looked down at the twisted handkerchief in her hands. "He has lost many friends over the last few years because of his angry outbursts, especially after he'd been drinking. The staff kept their distance from him because all have been witness to these eruptions, and most were unfortunately victims of his wrath."

Although it was difficult to say the words out loud, Amelia knew that after interviewing the staff this was probably not news to the inspectors. It was not something she was proud of, but she had always felt that honesty was indeed the best policy, and this situation should be no different.

Duffy and Shaw said their good-byes, bowed to the duchess, and left. Amelia stayed in the parlor, too worn out to move.

Rose, who had been standing behind her while she talked to the inspectors, asked, "Shall I retrieve you some hot tea and something to nibble on? You must keep up your strength, my lady, and you haven't eaten anything since breakfast."

"Thank you, Rose. A cup of tea would be nice, but I don't care to eat anything."

"If you don't mind, my lady, rather than call for a maid, I'll see to your tea myself. I'd like to keep busy."

"Of course, Rose. You go ahead. I'll be fine."

Rose quietly left the room to tend to the tea. And now that she was alone, Amelia found herself lost in thought. So many unanswered questions were running through her mind, and it seemed she was feeling a blend of emotions as well. She didn't know what to think or how to feel.

In the very beginning, she was afraid that a murderer was loose in the house, but she believed what she told the inspectors, that her husband's murder was his own doing. He had changed a great deal over the years and not for the better. *But who would dislike him enough to kill him?*

And if she were to be honest with herself, a part of her was a bit relieved. These past years had been very difficult, not knowing when he might appear from around a corner and what kind of mood he would be in when he did. She was constantly on edge, listening for his raised voice and wondering who or what had displeased him at that moment and if she would need to defuse any volatile situation. He is—or was—like a starving lion, ready to pounce on anyone who walked by.

But that still brought her back to the question of who would want him dead. Her mind flashed through the faces of those in the residence: Flanders, Parker, the groomsmen, and footmen. But one face kept coming back to her, the face of her son.

*Is it possible that a stubborn, precocious, eleven-year-old could be capable of murder? He obviously did not care for his father and had very little respect for him, but kill him?*

That seemed unimaginable, and yet she couldn't shake the nagging feeling that he might have hated his father enough to want him gone from their lives forever.

"Please, God. Don't let it be Herbert. Please don't let it be my son."

ᴌᴼ

Gatewood Castle was officially in a state of mourning. The mirrors in the house were draped in black crepe, and a large laurel wreath with black bunting was hung on the front door. Amelia would remain in mourning, wearing black clothing, for a year. A popular trend of the day was to keep a bit of hair from the deceased in a locket, but Amelia couldn't bring herself to do that. The man she was burying was not the man she had married. She had been privately mourning the loss of her husband for years and didn't feel that a relic like a wisp of hair would make her feel any better about the loss of the last years of their marriage or his death. If anything, it would be a reminder of his murder and the years leading up to that tragic point in his life. She'd rather try to concentrate on the early years and the happiness they shared before the drink and his anger took hold.

Amelia wrote notes to her father and to Leah and Emmons with the news. Her sister and brother-in-law arrived at the castle the next day with their trunks full of clothes, ready to stay for as long as they were needed. When Amelia saw them, she rushed to hug Leah and broke down sobbing. All the pain that Amelia had been trying to bury deep inside came bursting forth with each heart-wrenching sob. Leah gently placed a hand on the small of Amelia's back and led her into the nearby library. She sat cradling and rocking her on the settee as if Amelia were a little girl again.

All the while, Amelia cried until there were no tears left. "Oh, Leah, what a terrible thing has befallen this family." Amelia hiccupped into her handkerchief.

Leah reached out to grab Amelia's hands and turned to look steadily into her eyes. "Amelia, who did this? Who murdered the duke?"

"I do not know, sister. The police have talked to the servants, but I don't know that they have an answer as of yet."

Then very slowly Amelia took a deep breath. It was time to let go of the family secrets that she had kept hidden for nearly a decade. She told her sister and brother-in-law everything, starting with that terrible night on their honeymoon and how the drinking and anger had worsened over the years. She talked of how her husband would lash out and say terrible things to anyone who crossed his path, how he had beaten Herbert, and how he had tried to choke Amelia to death. Because of his verbal abuse, they had lost most of their friends and stayed away from the social functions they once enjoyed together. She talked of how their marriage had become a union in name only, that they rarely did anything together and had not had relations in the marriage bed in more years than she could count. It was like he had become the devil himself, and Amelia had tried but failed to make him see the error of his ways.

Finally Amelia finished her story. The tears had stopped flowing quite a while before, and after unburdening herself, she felt oddly relieved, as if a weight had been lifted from her shoulders. Leah and Emmons had quietly listened to the story for over an hour, occasionally shaking their heads in disbelief, but not uttering a sound.

"Amelia, I wish you had come to me sooner. Perhaps Emmons could have talked to him, making him see that he was in the wrong." Leah looked up at her husband, who had been sitting across from them in a leather wingback chair the whole time.

"Yes, Amelia. If I had known his temper had gotten that out of control, I would have put a stop to it immediately, one way or another, whether he would listen to reason. Or if necessary, I would have seen to it that he was sent away. Either way, I would not have let you carry this burden alone."

"I don't believe anything would have made a difference," Amelia explained. "I had many conversations with him about this, but he refused to listen. His melancholy and the pull of the drink were just too strong."

Her father arrived shortly after, and rather than go through the whole shameful tale all over again, she asked Emmons to repeat the story to her father. She found that she was exhausted and didn't have the energy to tell the tale for a second time. Everyone sat in the library clustered around Amelia until Emmons finished telling the story.

Her father could only shake his head. "Amelia, my dear, you have carried these burdens on your shoulders for too long. Why didn't you come to us? We could have helped you."

"Father, nothing could be done. I had tried many times to talk some sense into him, but he refused to listen. I kept hoping and praying that one day he might keep his promise to me and leave the drink. Instead he chose the drink over his family, and that was his undoing, but it was also his choice." She looked at her father as a single tear slid down her cheek.

"Woodford had fought his demons all his adult life, and those demons had been just too strong to overcome," Amelia said. "However, the question is not why he was killed. I think we can all theorize why. I need to know who did it, and as of now, I don't have the answer to that." Amelia kept her worries about her son to herself. It was too awful to say it out loud.

"Have the inspectors told you anything? Do they have a suspect?" As he spoke, Emmons started to walk toward the sideboard that held the brandy. He suddenly stopped in his tracks and turned back to the group. "I think I'll wait until later to have a drink."

"I spoke with the inspectors yesterday," Amelia continued. "They had talked to everyone who was here at the time, but they didn't seem to have any suspects. They said they would keep me informed."

The duke was laid out in the parlor for the viewing in a dark mahogany casket with flowers arranged all around the room. The day of his death, Amelia had asked Rose and Flanders to help wash and then clothe him in the suit he wore at their wedding. In his cravat, he wore the stickpin the children had given him at Christmas a few months before. Meanwhile, the kitchen staff was busily preparing the food that was offered to the endless parade of people coming to wish Amelia, Herbert, and Charlotte their condolences. Most of them seemed to express more concern that a murderer was at large than they did for the demise of the duke and probably came more out of curiosity than sorrow. In fact, very few of the visitors seemed truly upset that the duke was dead.

A large number attended the funeral service, but when Amelia took a closer look at the attendees, she realized they were there for her, not for her husband. He didn't have any remaining family outside Amelia and the children, but it appeared that he didn't have any friends either.

The chapel at Gatewood was filled to capacity with the family, the entire staff from Gatewood, and most of the staff members from her childhood home, Hartwell Manor. Not one mourner was there as simply a friend or associate to her husband, and Amelia felt her chest tighten with that realization. He had gone from being a friend to many to being a sad and angry loner. It was unfortunate but obvious that he had lost many friends and even made a few enemies in years past.

She also noticed that Duffy and Shaw were at the services. They had told her that, out of respect for the family, they would stay in the background so as not to disturb the events, but they would be at the chapel and cemetery, hoping to spot something that might point them to the identity of the murderer.

After the funeral services, the duke was interred in the family cemetery. A black lacquer funeral conveyance carried his coffin while the family rode together in the family carriage immediately behind the hearse. Emmons and Leah sat on one side of the carriage, while Amelia sat on the other with her children on either side of her. Charlotte had been very quiet and kept her eyes focused on her lap while Herbert stared out the window. Amelia would allow him the time to grieve in his own way, but she didn't like the fact that he seemed so distant.

*Did he not have any feelings of love toward his father at all?* She would have a talk with him soon to try to break down the icy wall that seemed to be surrounding his young heart.

At the graveside, the priest said a few words of prayer while the mourners listened quietly. When it was over, all walked back to the carriages, except for Amelia, who stayed behind. Her heart was breaking, not only because of her loss but also because of what would never be. She had always held out hope that he would give up drinking and come back to her as the man she had fallen in love with. Now that her dream would never come to fruition, she mourned the loss of the dream as much as the loss of the man.

She gently placed a gloved hand on his coffin and whispered, "I loved you, Woodford. I hope you are finally at peace, my love." She turned and walked slowly toward the carriage.

That night, Amelia lay awake in bed for hours. The night was very cold with thick clouds covering the moon and stars making the night as dark as pitch. Even with a warm fire in the brazier and thick blankets on top of her, she couldn't shake the cold that chilled her to the bone. The events of the last week kept playing over and over in her mind. *Why, Woodford, did you have to forsake your family for the drink? Did I, as your wife, not please you? What caused your melancholy?*

But the worst thoughts of all that plagued her mind involved Herbert and whether he was responsible for his father's death. She tried telling herself that Herbert couldn't possibly be the murderer.

He was too young, too innocent, and too good-natured to commit such a heinous crime. *No, he couldn't possibly have done it. Of course he didn't do it. It must have been someone else.*

Eventually, Amelia fell into a fitful sleep that horrible nightmares filled. One of the most vivid dreams was that Woodford had risen from the grave and was walking across the fields with clumps of mud clinging to the clothes he'd been buried in. His face was distorted in a grimace, his eyes glowed yellow like a wolf's, and his skin was so pale that it was almost blue. He kept calling her name, and she tried to answer him, yelling to him, but he would walk past her like she didn't exist. She would reach out to him and try to grab for his hand, but her reach was always too short. He turned away from her in death as he had in life.

The next night, Amelia lay in bed, hoping she would fall into a deep and dreamless sleep. But again, she lay awake for hours while her mind continued to churn. Eventually she fell asleep, only to have another nightmare. This time she dreamt that her son was chasing his father through the halls of Gatewood with the elephant bookend in his hand, raised over his head as if he were going to throw it at the elder man. They ran on and on, upstairs and downstairs, always running.

Amelia was standing in one of the halls, her feet frozen to the spot, trying to reach out to catch them as they ran past her, but just like the previous night's dream, she couldn't touch them. No matter how far she leaned toward them, she couldn't reach them, and the pursuit continued on and on, with Amelia helpless to do anything about it. She had tried so hard to stop the chase before Herbert could kill his father.

She awoke from the nightmare, drenched in sweat and shivering with fright. She tried to slow down her breathing by telling herself that it was only a dream. *Herbert did not kill his father, neither in the dream nor in real life. He did not kill his father.*

# Chapter 9

A few days after the funeral, Duffy and Shaw were going over their notes.

"Shaw, we're spinning our wheels and not getting anywhere. Perhaps we've overlooked someone." Duffy was tapping his chin with his finger as he spoke.

"Who do you have in mind?" Shaw raised an eyebrow at his partner's suggestion.

"It seems to me that young Herbert and his father did not have a close relationship. In fact, Woodford seemed to take great pleasure in embarrassing the lad in front of others whenever he had the chance."

"I see what you're saying." Shaw sat back and pondered that thought. "He didn't seem to care for his father at all. And he's quite a bit more grown up than most lads his age, so he could easily swing a heavy bookend."

"And his father wouldn't pay any attention to him if he were to enter the library when the duke was looking over the ledgers. He would simply ignore the lad, which would allow Herbert to approach the desk, grab the brass elephant, and hit his father with it," suggested Duffy.

"Yes," acknowledged Shaw. "Perhaps it's time we talked to the young duke."

That afternoon, Duffy and Shaw returned to Gatewood.

"If possible, we'd like to speak to the duchess," Duffy requested.

"I believe Her Grace is in her chambers. If you'd like to wait just a moment, I will ask Rose to get her." Flanders invited them in, took their hats and coats, and showed them to the parlor.

"Thank you, Flanders," the inspectors responded in sync.

Rose knocked quietly on the sitting room door. "Your Grace, Senior Inspector Duffy and Inspector Shaw are in the parlor. They would like to speak to you for a moment."

"Thank you, Rose. I'll be down momentarily. Please see that a tea tray and scones or tarts—whatever Cook made today—is brought to them."

Amelia looked at herself in the looking glass. Her face looked pale, and she had dark circles under her eyes. She pinched her cheeks in an attempt to add a bit of color, but it didn't seem to do much good. With a deep sigh, Amelia left her chambers and went downstairs to the parlor.

Duffy and Shaw had been sitting in the overstuffed chairs when Amelia, accompanied by Rose, appeared at the doorway. They immediately stood up and bowed as the ladies came in the room. Inspector Duffy reached out and took Amelia's arm to guide her to the sofa.

They exchanged the social niceties, commenting on the weather and such, while Rose poured tea for Amelia and the inspectors.

"How are you faring, Your Grace?" Amelia noticed the kindness in Duffy's eyes and the notion that he seemed truly concerned.

"I am as well as can be expected, I suppose. Thank you for asking, Inspector. That's very kind of you."

"Your Grace," said Shaw softly, cutting right to the chase, "we do have some questions for you, if you have a moment."

"Certainly, Inspector. What is it?"

"We noticed that there are what appear to be entries by two different people in the ledgers that were on the desk the morning your husband was killed. Whose handwriting is in those ledgers?"

"Well, Inspector, both my husband and I made those entries." Knowing that women were not supposed to be involved in business affairs, Amelia was a bit on the defensive and raised her chin a bit higher while she explained. "You see, my husband very often stayed at the townhome in London for very long stretches of time, rarely taking an interest in the running of the estate. Even after he returned here to Gatewood Castle, he had no interest in the business end of the estate. I was faced with the choice of either letting the estate go to ruin or making the decisions myself. Obviously the former was not an option, so I had no choice but to learn what I could about the farms and manage them accordingly. That, gentlemen, is why there are two different styles of handwriting."

Duffy, with a slightly raised eyebrow and a bit of a smile, gave her a nod, while Shaw continued to write in his notepad. Amelia could see that there was no judgment, only understanding, on their part. It made her feel better to know that they would not criticize her for what she felt she had to do, even if it did go against the rules of society.

Shaw continued, "We have to ask you as well where you were the morning your husband was killed."

Amelia drew in a deep breath to steady herself as she thought about that day. "The early morning hours are just as regimented for me as they are for anyone else, I suppose. I get dressed. Then I have a bit of something for breakfast with Herbert and Charlotte before they start their lessons, and then I spend the rest of the morning instructing the staff if they need direction or catching up on my correspondence. If the weather is nice, I might take a walk in the gardens or take a relaxing horseback ride to the north end of the estate.

"I don't believe that morning was different in any way. I had been in my sitting room going over some correspondence when I heard the commotion. I went downstairs to investigate when I saw the staff gathered in the hallway outside the study, and Flanders told me what happened."

Shaw looked at her intently. "Your Grace, did you kill your husband?"

"Absolutely not, Inspector." There was firmness in her voice as she spoke. "Most people never got to see the warm side of my husband. I consider myself very fortunate to have seen that he was a kind, loving, and gentle soul. That is to say, when he wasn't drinking. I loved my husband, Inspector, and would never have killed him."

"Did he ever hit you?" Shaw prodded.

"Yes, Inspector, he did. I'm not proud of that fact, but it is the truth." She looked down at her hands in her lap, trying to blink away the tears before they fell down her cheeks.

"Did he hit you often?" Duffy was trying to ask his questions softly, and Amelia could tell it was with understanding and compassion, hoping to show her that they understood it wasn't her fault.

"No, Inspector. I'll admit he had been physical with me a few times, but it was not often."

"We understand that he occasionally stayed in London," Duffy continued. "We also understand that there were periods when he stayed there for some length of time. Do you know what he was doing there?"

"No, Inspector. When he was no longer staying here at Gatewood, I had no contact with him unless he came back for some reason. Even then, I made a point of staying out of his way if he were in one of his moods. I suggest you talk to the gentlemen who frequent a pub in London called the Hammer and Sickle. I believe he went there quite often, so they are more apt to know of his activities while he was in London.

"And please feel free to look at the townhome while you're there, if you'd like. But I must say I don't know what condition it's in. No one in the family has been there these last few years except for him. He kept only a few household staff members as a necessity, and as I understand it, they were not allowed in his personal quarters."

"Your Grace, where might we find the servants from the town-home? Would you mind if we spoke to them?"

"Certainly, you may. I didn't see the point of letting them go just because the townhome is not being used at the moment, so rather than asking them to look elsewhere for employment, those staff members—a cook, a butler, and a housemaid—have all come here to Gatewood to work." Amelia gave a warm smile. "You see, Inspectors, in my family, we believe that there is always room for one more, and we're happy to have them here."

Both smiled at her in return.

"What are your plans for the townhome, Your Grace?" Shaw was inquiring.

She looked at him thoughtfully. "I honestly don't know, Inspector. I suppose, if Herbert isn't interested in keeping it, I would sell it, although I haven't looked into making those types of decisions yet."

"Your Grace, I'm sorry to say this, but we need to speak to Herbert as well. We'd like to ask the duke a few questions," Duffy said.

Amelia felt the color drain from her face and raised her eyebrows in surprise. She nodded her head in acknowledgement. "Of course, Inspector. He's with Mrs. Parker. I'll have Flanders get him for you."

A few moments later, Herbert came into the parlor.

"Son, would you like some tea?" asked Amelia in an attempt to act as normal as possible, making sure her nerves didn't show. Herbert declined the offer of tea but instead asked for a glass of milk. Rose left to get Herbert his drink.

"Your Grace, you and your father didn't really get along. Is that true?" questioned Shaw.

The young duke looked at the inspector with a wry grin. "You are correct, Inspector. My father and I didn't see eye to eye, to put it mildly."

"And why is that?"

"My father was a drunk and an evil drunk at that."

"Herbert!" Amelia brought her hand to her throat at the shock of her son's announcement. She quickly looked back and forth between her son and the inspectors, her cheeks turning red. "You shouldn't say things like that. He was your father after all, and he should be treated with respect."

"But, Mother, it's the truth. And he didn't care for anyone but himself, least of all me." He looked at the inspectors. "He had beaten me in front of others, humiliated me at every chance, and never had a kind word to say to me. It was worse when he'd been drinking, but of course, he was drunk more often than he was sober, so I was at the receiving end of his angry outbursts almost daily." As he sat there, Herbert was clenching and unclenching his fists.

"Where were you in the early morning hours on the day of your father's death?" asked Shaw.

"My day usually starts by taking Mayhem outside to do his business, followed by breakfast and then lessons with Mrs. Parker. That's where I was when Mother came in to tell Charlotte and me of his passing."

Duffy asked him, "How did you feel once you heard that your father had died?"

"You mean murdered? Honestly, I was not terribly surprised,

maybe a bit relieved. Like I said, he and I didn't see eye to eye, and he seemed to take pleasure in hurting people. He is at peace, and the world is a better place now that he's gone."

Amelia sat in stunned silence, listening to her son's admission as to how he felt toward his father.

"Thank you, Herbert—excuse me—Your Grace. We'll be in touch if we have any more questions."

As Herbert left the parlor, he held his head high but still clenched his fists at his sides. Rose was just returning and set the glass of milk on the tea tray since Herbert was no longer in the room. For proprieties' sake, she discreetly stayed with Amelia in the back of the room while the inspectors remained.

"My lady, we'd also like to talk to some of your servants again, if you don't mind," Shaw said. "We have some more questions for them."

"Certainly, you may. If it's easier, you may stay right here in the parlor, and I'll have them brought in to speak with you." Amelia spoke barely above a whisper as she tried to regain her composure. "Just let Flanders know who you'd like to see, and he will bring them to you. He's familiar with the servants and their schedules and will know where to find each of them."

Duffy and Shaw exchanged a glance at each other before Duffy spoke up. "Well, actually, Your Grace, he's the first one we'd like to talk to, if that's all right."

Amelia was a bit surprised at first but then realized that perhaps they only wanted information from him. He couldn't possibly be a suspect. "Feel free to do whatever you need to do, gentlemen. You have my permission to speak with whomever you'd like."

Amelia stood up to leave. The inspectors rose as she did.

"Good day, sirs." With that, she made her way into the hallway and then slowly up the stairs to her private chambers.

⌒⌒

Duffy had been watching Amelia as she left the parlor when he realized Flanders was standing right outside the doorway. He noticed the butler, with concern creasing his brow, was intently watching the duchess. Duffy gave a slight cough to get Flanders's attention.

Flanders shook his head as if to wake himself from his deep thoughts. "Yes, Inspector, can I help you with something?"

"We will be talking a bit more to a few of the servants, Mr. Flanders, and we'd like to start with you, if you don't mind. Would you step into the parlor, please?"

Duffy noticed a slight flicker in Flanders's eyes, but he stepped into the parlor with an otherwise unreadable expression. Rather than taking a seat, Flanders stood across from the inspectors as they sat down. Shaw tipped his hand in the direction of the sofa, indicating that Flanders should sit down. He continued to stand.

"Mr. Flanders, we know we've asked some of these questions already, but we'd like to go over it with you again." Shaw looked at his notepad as he spoke. "You previously said that, on the morning of the duke's death, you were in the kitchen with the other members of the staff having breakfast at about sunrise. Is that correct?"

"Yes, sir, it is."

"And then you spoke with the staff about their duties that day. Is that correct?"

"Yes, sir, that's correct." Flanders's expression never changed as he answered their questions. In fact, he looked almost bored with the interrogation.

"About what time was that?"

"I generally speak to the staff at eight o'clock. I don't believe that day was any different."

Duffy could sense the defiance building in the butler's

demeanor. He then asked, "Did the duke make a habit of working in his study every morning?"

"Yes, sir, he did. He had breakfast at seven o'clock, and by eight o'clock you could find him in the study."

Shaw continued asking, "What did he do when he was in the study?"

"I believe he handled the business of the estate, sir, but I'm not sure. He had always left strict instructions that he was not to be disturbed during that time."

"When did he come out of the study?"

"Usually by eleven o'clock, sir."

"Did you get the sense that he'd started drinking by then?"

"Yes, sir, as a matter of fact, he generally had already started drinking by the time he came out of the study. One of the maid's duties is to make sure the liquor bottles were always full, and she would replenish the bottles for the first time after he left and then throughout the day as needed whenever he returned."

"How long have you worked for the duke, Mr. Flanders?"

"I started out as a footman with the duke's father in my fifteenth year, and I am now in my fifty-fourth year, sir."

"How close are you to the duchess?"

Flanders immediately scowled at the investigators. "I'm not sure I like what you are implying, Inspector. I have worked for the duke's family for many years, but I'm not blind to his actions. I've watched him change over the years and become very abusive, especially to those closest to him. The duchess is a fine, honorable lady, and I did not care for the way he treated her. Rest assured, my fondness for Her Grace is unquestionably respectable, and I feel nothing untoward for her. I am, after all, almost old enough to be her father. Now, gentlemen, if you're through, I have work to do." He turned toward the door to walk out.

Duffy, ignoring Flanders's last comment, changed the course of the interrogation by asking, "Do you know who might have disliked the duke enough to kill him?"

Flanders stopped to turn back to the inspector and took in a deep breath. He slowly exhaled before answering, "A great many people did not care for the duke. He was quick to lash out at those around him when he was in a foul mood, especially when he was in his cups. Most people gave him distance because of it. But to dislike him enough to kill him? No, sir, I do not know who would do that." Flanders looked Duffy squarely in the eyes when he answered, and Duffy knew in his gut that he was either telling the truth or he was a damned good liar.

Duffy told him, "I would like to speak to Parker next."

The two investigators waited in the parlor while Flanders had a footman fetch Parker from the stables.

When he arrived, Parker seemed apprehensive. "Good day, gentlemen. How can I help you?" Parker sat in the chair opposite them, resting his cap on his knee.

"We'd like to go over a few things, if you don't mind," answered Duffy. "We had asked some of these questions the day of the murder, but please bear with us. We're trying to be thorough."

"Why are you bothering me with the same questions then? I have a lot of work to do."

Duffy quickly interjected, "We have some new evidence." This was a lie, but Parker didn't have to know that part. "We're just trying to piece it all together, and your cooperation will help a great deal."

Shaw got right to the point. "It was common knowledge among the other staff members that you had an intense dislike for the duke."

Parker nodded his head. "Aye, that's true. There's no denying that."

"Then why did you stay under his employ? You could have

gone elsewhere. We understand from some of the groomsmen that you have an impeccable reputation in caring for horses. Any one of the local estates would have hired you."

"The question," he explained, "is not *where* I would go. It's because I simply don't *want* to go. As you already know, my wife, Aubrey, is the children's governess. She is very fond of them, and they are equally fond of her. We were never blessed with children of our own, but she has come to think of Herbert and Charlotte as the next best thing. I might not have liked the duke, but Aubrey's love for the children is far greater than my dislike for the duke. And that, gentlemen, is why I've stayed."

"You were here the morning the duke was murdered, were you not?" Shaw continued.

"Yes, I was in the stables overseeing the feeding of the horses and cleaning of the stalls."

"And who was with you?" Duffy interjected.

"All of the stable hands were, sir. Six of them help me in the stables, and all six were at work that day. A couple of them are young lads, and unless I keep after them, their minds tend to wander, and the work isn't done properly. I like to remain on-site to make sure they stay to the tasks at hand."

Duffy and Shaw returned to police headquarters to go over the list of possible suspects. Flanders was a possibility because he seemed overly protective of the duchess. It was obvious he cared for Amelia a great deal, but they couldn't tell if it were improper. He was much older than she was, but he wouldn't be the first member of a staff to fall in love with the mistress of the house, regardless of an age difference. But they couldn't tell if she felt the same way toward him. That was something that would need to be investigated further, but neither one of the men felt this was the case with Amelia.

And because of his strong feelings against the duke, Parker

would remain a person of interest, even though they could not find the proverbial chink in his armor.

∽

Meanwhile, after leaving the inspectors to their work, Amelia had gone back upstairs to her chambers. Rose was in the sitting room, quietly dusting the furniture for the second time that week. The duke's death had greatly disturbed her as well, and she didn't seem to know what to do with herself.

"I seem to have a headache today, Rose. I think I'll lie down for a bit, but first I'd like to talk to Herbert. He's been so out of sorts. Would you mind finishing the dusting at another time?"

"Of course, Your Grace. Would you like a tray brought up? Perhaps some chamomile tea to help you relax?"

"No, thank you. But if you would be so kind as to ask Herbert to come in here, I would be grateful." Amelia put her hand on her chest, as if that would help ease the heaviness in her heart that she was feeling.

*This is not the way I thought my life would be,* she thought.

"Yes, Your Grace. Right away." Rose curtsied and left Amelia's chambers.

Amelia sat down in front of the window in her sitting room that overlooked some of the gardens. Although it was a beautiful view that she normally enjoyed, she wasn't able to enjoy the scenery today when she was so deep in thought. She wondered about the possibility of Flanders being the murderer. He had been under Woodford's employ the longest and had therefore seen the changes in the duke's demeanor over the years.

*It must have bothered him,* she surmised, as it troubled her to see him fall into such a deep well of despair. But the idea of Flanders killing the duke did not make sense. Amelia knew that Flanders was very fond of Woodford. Besides, Flanders rarely went into the study, and if he did, it was only to alert the duke that he had a visitor or give him his mail. *He certainly wouldn't have lingered in the study if Woodford were in there working.*

Next, she found her thoughts going to Parker. She was aware that Flanders and Parker had both been keeping a close eye on her for the last few months. It was a comfort to her, knowing that these two men had taken it upon themselves to secretly guard the children and her. She also was aware that he and Woodford had had a number of disagreements, and he didn't seem to care for the duke, but Parker had a gentle disposition. That was what made him so good when it came to caring for the animals on the estate. Amelia couldn't believe that anyone who was that kind and gentle could be capable of murder.

Rose found young Herbert sitting at his desk in his chambers, doing nothing but staring out the window. Mayhem was lying at his feet, but as Rose came to the door, the dog looked up, wagging his tail. With every wag came a light thudding noise as Mayhem's tail thumped against Herbert's leg. Rose gently knocked on the door, even though it was open.

"Excuse me, Your Grace." Rose spoke quietly. She had taken to calling him "Your Grace" since his father's passing because Herbert now carried the ducal title. "Your mother would like to see you in her chambers, if you please."

With a sigh, Herbert stood up. "Of course. Thank you, Rose."

She curtsied as he and Mayhem walked past her and turned down the hall to his mother's rooms.

"Hello, Mother. You sent for me?" He gave his mother a warm smile, always glad to see her.

"Ah, yes, Herbert. Please come in and sit with me for a bit. I'd like to talk to you." Amelia gestured toward the chair opposite hers and returned his smile.

He took a seat, with Mayhem lying on the floor next to him, and looked around the room that reflected his mother's fine taste in decorating. Herbert had always loved this room, not only because it reflected so much of his mother's tastes but also because it smelled lightly of lilac, his mother's favorite perfume. So much of her was represented in this room.

"There are some things I'd like to discuss with you," she began softly. "I know it hasn't been easy to come to grips with the fact that your father has died. I am also aware that you have not shared a closeness with him in many years, maybe more years than you can remember. But I want you to know that it wasn't always like this. When I first met your father, he was a dashing young man who made many young ladies' heads turn as soon as he walked in the room. We met at your Uncle Stanley and Aunt Leah's wedding and quickly fell in love. While we were courting and for a length of time after our wedding, we enjoyed each other's company tremendously. We laughed, we danced, and we had a grand time with our friends."

Herbert got up and walked to the window. He stood there quietly, looking out the window, listening closely to his mother.

"But as time went on, he became very melancholy and never seemed to be able to break away from that emotion. I believe his attempts to escape that feeling caused him to turn to the drink, but all that did was make him angry. It made no difference what I said or what anyone else said for that matter. He just couldn't shake the feeling of melancholy nor the whiskey. Eventually the drink ruled the man, not the other way around. And, Herbert, that truly was a waste because, without the drink, your father was a wonderful man. I know that he cared very deeply for you and Charlotte, but by the time you came along, he was already lost to the drink. I just want you to try to remember that he truly did love you."

Amelia had reached for Herbert's hands and held them tightly in her own, as if to reinforce what she was telling her son.

"I understand, Mother. I do find it difficult to believe, but I will try to remember what you've said."

"Thank you, Herbert. There's one other thing I need to discuss with you, that being your responsibilities as the new Duke of Brazelton. A tremendous amount of responsibility and hard work comes with the title. But you needn't worry about that quite yet. You won't reach your majority until your twenty-first birthday, and until that time, I will be here to help you. In fact, there was a time when I tended to the bookkeeping for the estate so I'm quite familiar. I'll be happy to show you what I've learned so you'll be ready when your time comes."

"Mother, forgive me, but how is it that you tended to the books of the estate? I didn't believe it to be proper for a woman to be so involved in the affairs of business."

"That is very true, Herbert, but there were times when your father had no interest in the estate, and I certainly couldn't leave it to rot, so I had no choice but to take over until he came to his senses. Eventually he would, but I've never forgotten what I'd learned." She leaned closer to him and whispered, "In fact, I quite enjoyed it."

She straightened up and continued, "Even when he was back to running the estate, I still peeked at the ledgers now and again, just to see how things were going." Amelia looked at her son with a crooked smile and raised an eyebrow, as if in a show of conspiracy now that he knew her secret.

"Actually, my son, although it is not spoken of in polite society, a great many women help their fathers, husbands, and sons behind the scenes in the affairs of business. Women are not necessarily the mindless ninnies men would like us to be."

Herbert managed a smile. "Mother, I've never thought you to be a ninny, that's for sure."

Amelia gave a gentle laugh at her son's compliment. "We must move forward, Herbert. The estate will not run itself, but as I've said, I am here to help you."

He kissed his mother on the cheek and left her to her rest.

The very next morning, Amelia began showing Herbert the intricacies of running the estate. He caught on very quickly as she showed him how to record the transactions in their respective columns in the ledgers. He was interested in the animals on the farms, especially in learning how to determine the number of sheep and pigs that could graze comfortably on an acre of grassland without overcrowding. He learned what crops were growing in the fields and how they should be rotated every year, keeping some fields fallow. Some crops would be used as feed for the animals, while others would be sold to neighboring estates as a lucrative income. He had no idea so much was involved, but he was truly enjoying it.

# Chapter 10

That same day, Duffy and Shaw were headed to London to make inquiries at the Hammer and Sickle but decided to head to the townhome first to see what they might be able to find there. As soon as they arrived, both looked out the carriage windows in shock. The outside of the townhome was in deplorable condition, overgrown with weeds and tall grass and strewn with garbage. A small metal fence on either side of the brick pavers leading to the front door was leaning over in spots because of the weight of the weeds pulling it toward the ground. The door and windows were desperately in need of fresh paint, and two of the shutters were hanging at odd angles. To the inspectors, it was obvious that no one had tended to the outside of the home in quite some time.

They descended the carriage steps and walked toward the front door. A field mouse scampered across their path, adding to the feeling of how overgrown the property was. Amelia had given them a key, which they used to pass through the front door and into the world of a man who had obviously gone mad.

The vestibule wasn't too bad, just dusty, from not being inhabited for so long. They found their way to the study, opened the door, and stopped in their tracks just inside the doorway. The drapes were closed so very little light was coming through, but it was enough to show the inspectors the state of disarray. The room smelled heavily of dust, dirt, and stale bourbon. At first glance, they could see the mound of papers on the desk and the tipped liquor bottles left on the credenza. Shaw went to one of the windows and opened the drapes to let in the sunlight, and when he turned to look back into the room, he could see it was even worse than they initially thought.

The partners looked at each other, shaking their heads, and through unspoken words, both knew that the duke had to have been living in this condition for a while. As they scanned the room, they could see the filth that covered every inch of surface. On his desk were piles of correspondence; ledgers with scribbled, nonsensical marks; old and unread newspapers; and a couple of dried-up inkwells. There were five or six tumblers on the desk as well, with a sticky-looking substance in the bottom of each one. The chairs were stained from spilled drinks, and the carpeting was filthy and stained as well. Amelia had said that the servants were not allowed in Woodford's personal quarters, and it was more than obvious that what she had heard was correct. The study hadn't been cleaned in many years.

They left the study and walked through the other rooms, but like the vestibule, they were tidy but dusty. The staff had at least tried to keep up appearances in the other, more public rooms of the townhome.

Duffy and Shaw found the duke's chambers upstairs, and as they looked around, they simply shook their heads in disbelief. The sitting room, dressing room, and bedchamber were in even worse condition than the study was. Dirty clothes littered the floor, bottles and glasses covered every inch of space on the tables and chests of drawers, and the bed had a dirty pile of what were probably sheets and a blanket heaped in the middle. The stench of dust, dirt, and stale body odor was so bad that both Duffy and Shaw had to hold a handkerchief to their noses. They quickly closed the door to his chambers and left the townhome, locking the front door behind them. It was clear to them that nothing in the duke's home had been disturbed in quite some time, so they would find nothing related to his murder there. The only thing it confirmed was the state of the duke's mind in the years leading up to his murder.

The next stop was at the Hammer and Sickle, about four blocks from the townhome. Both Duffy and Shaw were grateful for the few minutes it took by carriage to reach the tavern because it gave them a chance to air out their clothing and their noses. However, when they entered the tavern, they realized the air wasn't much better in there than it was at the study in the townhome. The Hammer and Sickle was dark and dank, reachable only by stairs that led below ground because of its location in the basement of a small, brick building.

Above ground, the building was comprised mostly of clothing and cigar shops for what appeared to be men of the middle class. The shops did not seem to have the quality of goods that would interest the upper class, men like the duke. So they pondered: why did the duke frequent this tavern? Perhaps because it was so close to the townhome?

The inspectors decided that the best plan of action would be to order a couple of drinks and try to observe what they could before they started asking questions. Each ordered a glass of ale at the bar and then took their seats at an empty table in the corner, positioning themselves so they could watch the other patrons. Most of the men in the tavern drank quietly and alone, while a couple of them conversed with the barmaid, who was going from table to table every few minutes, offering to bring the men more drinks. It didn't seem like a bad place, but they felt they were correct in their initial assessment that it didn't seem to be the kind of place that gentlemen of the upper class would frequent.

Eventually the barmaid made her way over to Duffy and Shaw. She was a round woman of about forty-five years old with wild graying hair. She was wearing a well-worn and stained blouse that struggled to cover her ample bosom. Her corset, worn over the blouse, appeared to be at least two sizes too small, but because it had to be laced loosely, she wore a thick belt at her waist to hold it all in place. Her skirt was tattered at the hemline, and her apron was so gray and dingy that the inspectors doubted it had ever been white.

"Can I get you anything?" She gave the younger Shaw a suggestive smile and winked.

Shaw returned the grin. "What's your name, darlin'?"

"My mum named me Mathilda, but folks 'ere call me Tilley. And what's yours?"

"My name is Shaw, and this is Duffy. Do you mind if we ask you a couple of questions?"

"That depends." They could see her stiffen as she answered. "Are you coppers?"

Duffy interjected, "Yes, we're inspectors, and we're investigating the Duke of Brazelton's murder. We know he came here quite often. Is there someone here who might have known him that we can talk to?"

"Aye, the barkeep is your best bet. Most people 'ere dinna have much use for Woodford. He always thought he was better than us, he did, but if he was so much better, how come he came to a place like this at all?" With a loud *humph*, Tilley walked back to the bar to speak to the bartender.

Duffy and Shaw gave each other a glance as the barmaid turned her back on them. They watched as she had a conversation with the bartender, who scowled at them from over her shoulder. He'd been wiping a glass with a towel, but he set the glass on the bar, wiped his hands with the cloth, and made his way to their table.

"You was askin' about Woodford?"

"Yes, we're investigating his murder." Duffy and Shaw stood up to shake his hand. It was better to appear friendly and less official to try to put the man at ease.

"I don't know nuffin' about that. The man come in here to drink, and that's all I know."

"We understand that he was a heavy drinker and he got very mean when he drank." Duffy stopped so the bartender would pick up the thought from there.

"Yeah, he drank a lot. But I dinna mind taking his money, so what do I care?"

"We understand that he got himself into quite a few fights." Duffy was trying to convey that the responsibility for the duke's behavior was his own.

"Aye, that he did. The man dinna know when to keep his mouth shut. The regular customers knew to give him a wide berth, but if someone new came in, the duke started picking at him until a fight broke out. It wouldn't have been so bad if he'd won a fight once in a while, but the man just dinna know how to fight. He lost every time." The barkeep shook his head, but at the same time, he had a bit of a smile as if he enjoyed fights.

"Who did he pick a fight with? Anyone in particular?" Duffy was still looking for suspects.

"Nah, just the sorry blokes that happened to wander in. Most of the time, they dinna come back after getting into a fight with a duke. Afraid of gettin' arrested, they was."

"Do you know why he preferred to come here rather than an establishment like Almack's?"

The man glowered at Shaw for asking that question. "Do ya think we're not good enough for the likes of him?"

"Not at all," Duffy explained. "But you must admit that a man like the duke doesn't ordinarily come to a tavern like this on a regular basis, and as we understand it, he preferred the Hammer and Sickle to any other establishment."

The man puffed out his chest with a sense of pride. "That's because he preferred to drink at a quiet place where other people wasn't nosin' into his business. He came in, sat at the table that you're at now, and would drink his fill without being bothered. Except for pickin' the occasional fight, he kept to hiself, and he dinna bother us, so we dinna bother him. 'Ave a good day, gentlemen." And with that, the bartender turned on his heel and went back to the bar.

"Well," Shaw said, "it looks like our list of suspects just increased. We'll need to talk to some of the men in the area and find those he fought with. Maybe one of them went to Gatewood Castle to finish the job."

Early that evening, Shaw had gone home to be with his family, but Duffy returned to Gatewood to talk to Amelia. He knocked on the front door, knowing it was a bit late in the day for an unexpected call. Flanders reluctantly let him in and showed him to the parlor before leaving to summon Amelia. Duffy had secretly hoped that he would find her in.

"I apologize, Your Grace, for stopping in at such a late hour, but I wanted to discuss a few things with you, if you have a moment."

"Of course, Inspector. What can I help you with?" She motioned for him to have a seat in one of the chairs.

Duffy noticed that Amelia was looking better than she had appeared in the last couple of months. She didn't seem to be as pale as she was right after the loss of her husband, and he was glad to see her health improving.

When he had first come to Gatewood on the day of the murder, he had noticed the beautiful embroidered picture hanging on the wall. "That's a beautiful piece, Your Grace. Did you stitch that?"

"Yes, I did. I must admit that it looks nice here in the parlor, where it's a bit sunnier and shows off the colors better. I fashioned it after an area here on the estate. A creek runs along the eastern edge of the property, and it widens out just a bit in that spot. In the early mornings, the sun reflects off the water, and it's just beautiful. The water is so peaceful and tranquil there. It's one of my favorite places on the entire estate."

She had a warm smile as she spoke of her favorite spot, and he could see how pretty she was when she smiled. It made him happy after all she'd been through in the last few months to see her smile.

"But you didn't come here to listen to me ramble on and on about creeks and needlework. What can I help you with, Inspector?"

"Well, Your Grace, you had mentioned that it's been a long while since you've been to the townhome, and I wanted to let you know of its condition."

"Oh, dear. I was afraid of this. How bad is it?"

"Nothing that a bit of elbow grease wouldn't cure, but I do feel it should be tended to as soon as possible. It doesn't appear that anyone has been inside in quite some time, but if left unattended for much longer, it's apt to draw attention from vandals. In fact, I'm surprised it hasn't already. The front yard is overgrown by weeds and will need some tending to, along with some fresh paint on the outside walls. If that were done, it should help to dissuade any thugs or street urchins from considering it a vacant home. Then the inside can be worked on without drawing any further attention."

"Well, Inspector, I certainly appreciate your advice and will see to this immediately. I think I'll send Parker first thing in the morning. He can bring along a couple of the groundskeepers to start working on the yard and maybe a couple of housemaids to start with the dusting and cleaning inside. In the meantime, Inspector, we were just sitting down to dinner, and you are most welcome to join us."

Duffy stood up as Amelia rose. "That's very kind of you, Your Grace. I would love to."

Cook had prepared a delicious meal of roasted duck, one of the best Duffy had ever tasted. As a bachelor, he relied mostly on meals he picked up from the local shops on the way home, so it was a rare treat to have a meal that tasted as good as this.

The conversation among Duffy, Amelia, Herbert, and Charlotte was light and pleasant. They talked of the children's studies, the crops and animals in the fields, and the politics of the day, but nothing to do with the duke or the murder. The time passed quickly, and before he realized it, the time had come for Duffy to leave. It wasn't very often that he pined for being a family man, but after nights like tonight, he could see what he was missing.

Flanders gave Duffy his hat and coat, and he turned to Amelia, Herbert, and Charlotte and gave them all a genuine "thank you" with a small bow. And with a contented smile and a full belly, he headed home.

# Chapter 11

In the weeks since his father's passing, young Herbert became more outgoing and less withdrawn, and his eyes developed a sparkle that Amelia hadn't seen in many years. Slowly, bit by bit, the icy wall that Herbert had put up when his father was alive came crumbling down. He had taken to riding across the farms of the estate on Pegasus, with Mayhem running alongside, to observe as much of the land as he could. Amelia was watching her son come out of his shell, and she was very proud of him.

Charlotte had done her share of transforming as well. Instead of skulking around corners, she ran through the halls, light as air, knowing she had nothing to be afraid of. Where before she was so skittish that she avoided making eye contact with people, now she was anxious to talk with everyone, and when the opportunity presented itself, she would climb onto laps for a bit of personalized attention. It was almost as if she were making up for lost time, trying to get as much attention as she could.

Amelia's children couldn't be any more different from each other. Herbert was cautious and pensive, slow to react because he preferred to think first and act later. He was more comfortable being on the outside as an observer, taking everything in, but he was also very black and white about those observations and honest in his convictions. He seemed to have a bit of a temper and could be quick with a comment when he was passionate about something.

Charlotte, on the other hand, became very outgoing and loved the attention. She was lighthearted and couldn't bear sadness. She would do her best to spread happiness to everyone she encountered and liked holding hands as a way to spread that happiness to those around her. Amelia thought of her as a butterfly, flitting to and fro, bringing a smile to everyone's lips.

The staff seemed to have a lighter step in their walk and held their heads a bit higher. They no longer looked at the floor as they walked in the hallways. And although she was clothed in black, as propriety dictated, Amelia even felt her own demeanor improve. Overall, the heavy atmosphere had brightened tremendously at the estate in the last few weeks. Amelia was happy to see the changes, especially in her children, but it was hard to accept that it was at the cost of her husband's life. A small part of her would never again be whole.

An arrest had still not been made in the murder of the duke. Duffy and Shaw returned to Gatewood several times to continue their investigation, but no new evidence had surfaced. Both felt they were missing something but couldn't put their finger on it. Something was niggling at them both, but they didn't know what it was.

Whenever they returned to the estate, Duffy and Shaw would reinterview some of the members of the staff in the hopes that something would jump out at them. But no one's testimony wavered, and no new facts were divulged.

Flanders proved to be a valuable resource in that he was a link to the servants, especially the ones who were hesitant to talk to the inspectors. But even Flanders was unable to come up with anything new.

As the investigation progressed, Parker remained a person of interest in the case, primarily because he had such an intense dislike for the duke. But was his hatred for the duke enough to propel him to commit murder? Regardless of their gut feelings, they couldn't find the evidence that would point to him as the murderer.

Unfortunately Amelia was also considered a possible suspect. After all, she had the most to gain through her son's inheritance. Amelia, an abused and neglected spouse, certainly would not have been the first woman to kill her husband. However, she seemed extremely distraught over Woodford's death, and Duffy believed in his heart that she was not capable of murder.

One afternoon, about a month after the duke's death, Duffy and Shaw returned to Gatewood Castle in their constant struggle to solve the crime. A footman opened the heavy double doors, allowing them entry into the foyer. Flanders was there before either inspector had a chance to give his cloak to the footman.

"Good afternoon, Inspectors. What can I help you with?"

"Hello, Mr. Flanders," said Shaw. "Any news for us?"

"Nothing, sir. Nothing at all, but I keep hoping that something will come up."

Duffy had a thought. "Shaw, let's go back into the study and look around again. Maybe we've missed something in there. I just can't seem to shake the feeling that there is something right in front of our noses that we're missing."

"I feel the same," said Duffy. "It wouldn't hurt to have yet another look."

They headed toward the study, meeting Amelia and Rose along the way.

"Good day, Your Grace. Good day, Rose," the inspectors said.

"Good day to you as well." Amelia smiled. "Where are you off to today, Inspectors?"

"We thought we would go back to the study," Duffy told her.

"We both feel that we're missing something. Something that's right in front of our noses, but we can't quite come up with it. We've talked to everyone involved until we're blue in the face, but we thought perhaps if we go back to the scene of the crime, maybe we'll find what we're searching for."

"Is there anything I can do to help?"

"Not at the moment, Your Grace, but we appreciate your offer. We will keep you apprised of any progress we've made." The inspectors both tipped their heads and turned toward the study.

Suddenly Duffy stopped and turned back to Amelia. "Your Grace," he called out to her.

Amelia and Rose turned to look back at the inspectors.

"Nothing, Your Grace. Never mind. Thank you."

Duffy grabbed Shaw by the sleeve. "Come on, Shaw. We need to go back to the office."

"What's the matter?"

"I need to check something first, but I might have just figured out what we've been missing. If I'm right, I know who murdered the duke."

# Chapter 12

An hour later, the inspectors returned to Gatewood Castle. When Flanders met them at the door, they asked to see him, Amelia, Herbert, and Rose in the parlor.

Flanders found the duchess in her chambers with Rose. Amelia was writing letters while Rose worked on her sewing.

"The inspectors are back, Your Grace, and would like to see you, Herbert, Rose, and myself in the parlor."

"Of course, Flanders. We'll be right there."

Amelia made her way downstairs with Rose, while Flanders and Herbert followed a moment or so after.

"Good afternoon, gentlemen. You wished to see us?" Amelia took a seat on the sofa. Her son took the seat next to her after he came in, while Rose and Flanders stood behind them. "Rose, would you see that a tray is brought for the inspectors, please?"

"No, thank you," Duffy responded politely. He hesitated for just a moment. "We have some important news for you. We believe we have discovered who killed your husband, Your Grace."

Amelia's hand went to her chest. Her eyes grew wide, and she could feel the blood drain from her face at the news. "Dear Lord. Please tell me who did this. Who killed my husband?"

Duffy reached into his pocket and pulled out a small, white seedling pearl. He held up the pearl for everyone to see. "I found this on the morning of the murder on the duke's back. If you'll remember, the duke was found lying facedown on the floor."

Amelia closed her eyes as she pictured her husband as he lay there dead. "Yes, Inspector. I very much remember."

He looked at Amelia. "I'm sorry to paint this image for you, Your Grace, but it's important to understand that the only way it could have been on his back was if it landed there *after* he was killed. We know for a fact that the only two people who entered the room after your husband were the maid who discovered the body and the killer. The maid only made entry into the room as far as the doorway. She never made it past the threshold, and we checked with her a few minutes ago. She doesn't own any jewelry that has pearls this size, and Flanders confirmed that he'd never seen her wearing pearl jewelry. It wasn't until today when I called to you in the hallway that I looked closely at Rose's brooch. It was then that I saw it was missing a small pearl, one that is the same size as the one I hold in my hand. The same size as the one that was found with the duke after he'd been killed."

Rose's hand instinctively went to the brooch that was pinned to the neckline of her dress.

The young duke stood up while Amelia looked from Rose to the inspectors and back again. "Rose? Rose, is this true? Did you kill my husband?"

Rose looked down at her hands, twisting them one over the other, avoiding her mistress's eyes. The tears were running down her cheeks. "Yes, my lady. Yes, I did. I'm so sorry to have caused you so much pain. You, His Grace, and Lady Charlotte." She was sobbing now, so much so that the words came out as little more than a whisper.

"But, Rose, I don't understand. Why would you do such a thing? Why?" The tears welled up in Amelia's eyes.

"My lady, I have been your lady's maid—nay—your friend for many years. It broke my heart to see him hurt you in so many ways, so many times. He was a very cruel man. He was cruel to his family and even more so to the servants. No one was safe, neither man nor beast!"

Rose was raising her voice, talking through clenched teeth. "He was always angry and taking that anger out on all of us. If we passed him in the hall, he'd scream at us for no reason at all. If he didn't see anyone, he would tug on the bellpull, and whoever answered his call would catch the duke's wrath. It seemed that he would summon us for no other reason than to have someone to yell at! And it didn't stop at just the yelling. Sometimes he would hit us … all of us. It's been that way for years, and it was only getting worse."

She finally looked at Amelia. "I'm sorry I didn't tell you about the effects of his anger on the servants, but you had enough burdens to carry, and I didn't want to add to them. You couldn't have done anything anyway. You had tried to talk to him about his drinking a number of times, but he wouldn't listen. It was getting so bad that I thought about leaving. Oh, I wanted to leave, to be sure. Run, and never come back. But I wouldn't leave you, Your Grace. I was afraid for you, for His Grace Herbert, and Lady Charlotte, and that's the truth of it. I'm sorry his loss hurt you, but I'm not sorry that he's dead."

Amelia stood up and walked toward Rose, and they looked at each other for what seemed a long time, but was actually only a few moments. Finally Amelia wrapped her arms around Rose and hugged her tight. Rose was sobbing into Amelia's shoulder, but the duchess had tears running down her cheeks as well.

"Oh, Rose. I'm so sorry. I'm so sorry he treated you that badly." Amelia could barely get the words out.

Duffy and Shaw had been observing the exchange without interrupting. But now it was time for some answers.

Shaw spoke up. "Can you tell us what happened that morning, Rose?

Rose drew in a deep breath and tried to compose herself. She wiped her eyes and blew her nose with a handkerchief she'd pulled from a pocket of her uniform. It had been one of a beautifully stitched pair that Amelia had given her the Christmas before.

"He was in the study, as he was every morning. He had summoned for a servant, so I went to see what he needed. Normally Flanders would go, but that morning, Flanders was already occupied with something else. Apparently I took longer to get to the study than His Grace thought I should have because he was very angry by the time I got there. He started yelling at me, cursing and saying foul, nasty things. He was saying things that no lady should have to hear. I'm so sorry, Your Grace. I just couldn't take it anymore. I wanted it to stop. I wanted his foul mouth to stop spewing such vulgarities. I picked up the bookend, and I hit him with it. Only once, but I hit him with it."

Rose buried her face in her hands, her shoulders heaving as she sobbed.

"What happens now, Inspectors?" Amelia felt drained, as if everything around her were spinning. Her world was spinning and spinning like a whirling dervish, and she couldn't get it to stop.

Inspector Shaw deferred to Senior Inspector Duffy, the more experienced of the two. "I'm sorry to say this at such a time, Your Grace, but the duke had a very dark reputation. It was well known that he had a fiery temper, and many witnesses will attest to that fact. Because of that, I believe, if we talk to the magistrate, he may see fit to go easy on Rose."

"Thank you, Inspector. If possible, I would like to propose that Rose continue staying on here at Gatewood Castle. I will personally vouch for the fact that she will remain here on this property until we hear from the magistrate. I give you my word." Amelia put her hand protectively around Rose's shoulders while the housemaid kept staring down at the floor, the tears wetting her cheeks.

"Wait!" Herbert spoke up. All eyes turned toward him. He stood up and walked toward Rose and his mother. "I can't let you take the blame, Rose. I killed him. I killed my father."

"What did you say?" Amelia looked at her son, not believing what she had just heard. Amelia's hand, which had been holding Rose's shoulder, now went to her own throat.

Inspector Duffy looked first at Shaw and then at Herbert. "Your Grace, would you tell us what happened?"

"I was heading outside that morning with Mayhem when I saw Rose leaving the study. She looked terribly upset. I called to her, but she never even heard me." Herbert looked at Rose. "The door was open, and when I looked in, Father was lying on the floor. I saw the bookend next to him. I picked it up, held it high over his head, and let it drop. I left the study, but this time, I made sure the door was closed behind me."

"Oh, Herbert." Amelia rushed to her son. She wrapped her arms around his shoulders in a hug.

Herbert's arms fell limply to his side.

"Your Grace, do you know if your father was still alive at the time that you were in the study?" Duffy asked. "Was he moving, or did he say anything to you?"

"No, Inspector. He wasn't moving, and he didn't say anything."

Amelia felt like her legs would give way at any moment and she would collapse to the floor. "Inspector Duffy." She was speaking just barely above a whisper. "I don't know what to say or think. What will happen now?"

"My lady, this is indeed a turn of events. We'll have to discuss this with the magistrate."

Duffy motioned to Shaw with a tip of his head that it was time to go.

⌒

Two days later, Duffy and Shaw returned to Gatewood Castle to meet with Amelia, Herbert, and Rose. Flanders showed them into the parlor before summoning the others.

Within a few minutes, all gathered to hear what news the inspectors might have and what information they carried from the magistrate.

Shaw held his hat in his hands, gently running his thumbs over the brim. "We've spoken to the magistrate, and he said he personally knew the duke. The magistrate was fully aware of the duke's reputation, drinking, and anger issues."

"The situation is further complicated because two people are involved in his death," Duffy continued. "However, there is no way of knowing who is directly responsible for his death. That is, which blow to his head is the one that killed him. The magistrate felt that it would be unfair to charge two people in a crime when one might not be guilty. The magistrate has also agreed that, because of the duke's violent temper and physical outbursts toward everyone in this household, there is a good argument in this situation for self-defense. Herbert and Rose, no charges will be levied against either one of you."

Amelia first ran to Herbert, wrapping her arms tightly around him. They quietly cried in each other's arms. Next, Amelia went to Rose, her personal maid, her friend, and her confidante. They clung to each other as the tears continued.

The inspectors let themselves out.

# About the Author

LeeAnne James lives in central New York with her husband, their son, and the family dog. By day, she works as an administrative clerk to the chief of police in a local police department. In her spare time, she is an avid reader but also enjoys cooking, baking, and spending time with her family. *Murder at Gatewood* is her first novel.